Tales to Read in a Hammock

Robyn P. Murray

Copyright © Robyn P. Murray 2013

Robyn P Murray asserts the moral right to be identified as the author of this work.

A catalogue record for this book is available from the
National New Zealand Library

ISBN 13: 9780992263706
ISBN: 0992263700
Publisher: Robyn P Murray Hirst New Zealand

INTRODUCTION
LEAVING DANNY
MARNIE AND JOE COMING HOME
THE GIRL WHO WAS FOUND IN A SEA GULL'S NEST
WHERE DID YOU GET THOSE EYES?
PAROS
THE WELL-TRAVELLED SUITCASE
MORNING ROUNDS: MRS. JONES
BANANA SPLIT
THE TWIG
THE UNFINISHED DANCE
MOONLIGHT AND MEMORIES
WEEKEND IN RUSSELL

All rights reserved. No part of this publication may be reproduced, stored in a retrieval system, or transmitted by any form or by any means, electronic, mechanical, photocopying, recording or otherwise, without the prior permissions of the author and publishers.

Introduction

These stories were written over a number of years, and several have been read on the radio programme *Writers on Air*.

Some have been published in magazines others were tasks set by the writers' group I belong to, or I overheard a conversation and thought it would make a good tale.

The types of stories I have written, I hope, are similar to those by some of my favourite authors whose novels I have read many times. If you can find a book or an author you enjoy reading and, when finished, are left wanting to know "'what happens next,'" then that, for me, is a sign of a good story.

Some of these stories have been sitting on my shelves for years. Though some stories are destined to become novellas, I decided to publish this collection in the interim. Because I am completing another collection which is set from 1914 to the present day and is taking a little longer to finish than I thought, I would like to make *Tales to Read in a Hammock* available for summer; these tales go nicely by a log fire too.

Leaving Danny

It was ten past six on a cold wet winter evening when Maureen left Danny. She remembered the time particularly as she was straphanging on the bus. Her eyes level with the watch of a tall young man whose hand was above hers, holding onto the pole midway along the bus.

Suddenly the bus driver slammed on the brakes; a cyclist weaving through the traffic had cut across his path. Everyone standing lurched forwards and the bags of groceries that Maureen was clutching that she'd rushed to pick up during her lunch hour for dinner, fell on the floor and disappeared under seats. It was the proverbial straw that broke her stoic reserve of strength to keep on coping.

"Stop the bus!" she yelled. Leaving the bags of fruit, vegetables, and chicken where they were, she pushed her way to the door, ignoring the stares of other passengers, some sympathetic, some disapproving. She clambered off the bus and watched as it disappeared in the rain and traffic. "I can't do this anymore."

She was standing outside a small pub, whose lights spilt invitingly onto the wet pavement. Pushing her way through the door, she found a warm, cozy room where a fire burned and people murmured quietly relaxing at the end of their working day. Walking over to the fireplace, she sat down on an old settle and stretched her sodden feet towards the heat.

"Like a drink, love?" said a young woman, who was clearing glasses and wiping tables.

"Mmm! Yes, please - I'll have an Irish coffee, hot and strong,"

"Coming up," said the waitress cheerily, "Anything to eat? Garlic bread nibbles…?"

"Thanks, whatever's handy."

Her mind was still a blank. Maureen had gotten into the habit of pushing her thoughts away, coping only with whatever had to be done in the next hour or day for Danny and the children. Only when she was at work in the City Planning Department did she feel she was part of the real world.

The young waitress put a steaming mug of Irish coffee and a platter of bread, dips, and cheese in front of her with a smile. "There you are, love, that should warm you up."

"Thank you," said Maureen gratefully. She felt the warming coffee slip down her throat and her feet coming back to life. Somehow Maureen felt different, better than she had felt for a very long time. Although her hair was dripping down her neck and her wet clothes stuck to her body, for some reason she wasn't stressing that she wouldn't be home in time to prepare dinner.

For Danny sitting reading the paper, Vanessa slouched in front of television chewing her hair and endlessly texting her friends, Bryan hypnotized in front of his Xbox games. None of them would have thought to start preparing dinner or put washing on. Their coats and bags would be lying in the hall where they dropped them. They'd just be sitting and waiting for Maureen to call them for dinner when it was ready.

A sudden thought entered Maureen's head; *"I've left Danny."* She paused, wondering where that thought had come from; then realized that was exactly what she had done. She didn't feel guilty, just detached. Relief and a little fear rushed through her body as she thought back over the last seventeen years. How had she become so cowed and browbeaten, her confidence gone? Life now was…nothing. She was living in a vacuum, at the beck and call of her demanding family. How had she become such a victim?

The evening went on, and in the home Maureen had created for the three people who sat waiting, they suddenly realized that something was different. There was no smell of dinner being prepared, no noise from the kitchen. The lights hadn't been switched on, and as usual they were waiting to be called for dinner while watching whatever was showing on TV.

"Hey, where's Mum?" said Bryan, "I'm hungry, and I need my kit to go out to karate."

"I didn't hear her come in," said Vanessa, "and I need my costume for the dress rehearsal of the play tonight."

Danny looked up and said crossly, "Well, why aren't you getting your gear ready?" He had a moment of frisson wondering where Maureen was, then said angrily, "She is probably helping them out in that stupid office. Very inconsiderate, I'm going out myself later."

"But she would have phoned," said Vanessa. They all looked at each other with a faint feeling of unease. But nobody phoned the office to check if Maureen had left for the evening, and no one moved to organize something to eat or sort out their kit.

A little later a taxi drove up. Maureen turned the key in the lock and strode inside. Three accusing faces glared at her, "We haven't had our dinner! We need our stuff," said the kids in unison.

"It's not good enough, Maureen," Danny put in." I am supposed to be meeting other managers from out of town to discuss strategy for next quarter."

"Oh, dear!" said Maureen, "Don't you mean you are going down the pub, Danny? There is plenty of bread in the freezer and eggs on the bench top. You could have made something for yourselves. Bryan and Vanessa, did you get your gear for me to sort out at the weekend? Of course not! As usual, you leave everything for me to organize at the last minute. It is not my fault if they are not ready."

Three sets of jaws dropped.

Hanging her coat up, Maureen picked up her bag and climbed the stairs, saying over her shoulder, "I've eaten, I'm going upstairs to have a long hot soak in the bath, and then I will hop into bed; in the spare room, Danny. I want to read my library book, and I know how annoyed you get when the light is on."

For once the whining stopped. Shocked, nobody could think of anything to say.

Turning at the top of the stairs, Maureen said firmly, "Breakfast will be on the table at nine o'clock tomorrow. It's Saturday morning, so you don't have to rush off, no school or work. I want to let you know about some decisions I've made. Life as we know it is about to change. Don't be late!" Without waiting for a reply, she turned and closed the bathroom door firmly behind her.

Still standing at the bottom of the stairs in disbelief, trying to take in what Maureen had said, Danny and the children heard the sound of bath water running, then the smell of bath salts drifting out and the unusual sound of singing.

Later, Maureen snuggled down in the spare bed, a tray of tea on the bedside table, Wilbur the old cat tucked purring under her arm, hot water bottles at her back and feet, and library book at hand. She thought over the events of the past few hours and how it seemed her life had changed forever. She wasn't quite sure what she was going to say to her family tomorrow at breakfast, but she knew with certainty that her life was changing for the better. She hoped eventually her family would come to feel the same.

That silly sod on the bicycle will never know how he saved my life by almost causing an accident when he cut in front of the bus, she thought, grinned to herself, snuggled down, picked up her book, and began to read.

—First published in *Her Business and Lifestyle Magazine*, and read on *Writers on Air*

Marnie And Joe Coming Home

Two figures stood motionless on the deck of the holiday home where they were staying, watching for the familiar predawn view of the beach at the bottom of the hill. It was the first day of the New Year, and two old friends were enjoying a favourite place and time of day for their holiday together.

They tried to spend their holiday together every year, but as time went on and they both became more successful in their careers and lives, another year often slipped by before they knew it. This year, by chance or good luck, they were both in New Zealand at the same time.

The rising sun shot fingers of gold, illuminating the water and sand. Suddenly, as though an artist had dipped his brush in rose pink and drawn it along the white foam, the edges of the crashing surf were no longer white but a delicate pink. As the sun climbed higher from behind the hills, the beach was filled with a glorious light.

"A photographer is never around when a picture like that unfolds." Joe smiled at Marnie, and they sat at the table on the deck to breakfast on fruit, bread warm from the oven, and coffee.

Marnie and Joe had met as students enrolled in a Media Studies course in Christchurch almost twenty-five years ago. They'd found in each other a soul mate; both were determined to succeed and encouraged each other when their Tutors urged them to make more effort. They were ambitious, and each had a passionate determination to excel and make a difference. They both worked hard and strived to be the best in their group.

After graduating, Joe left to take a scholarship in London before being offered a prime opportunity with Reuters News Agency in Germany. Marnie's Tutor, recognizing her talent, suggested she freelance for newspapers in

Australia and New Zealand. When she had really learned her craft, she was commissioned to offer opinion and insight for media around the globe. Working hard over the years, gaining experience and knowledge, they both earned highly respected awards and accolades from their peers.

Joe and Marnie kept in touch, meeting when their busy schedules allowed, but somehow they were never in the same place long enough to take their relationship to the next level. In the end they both made a pact that they would meet annually, either the last week of the year or the first week of the New Year. They had a favourite spot in New Zealand in the Bay of Plenty, where they had spent many University vacations swimming, talking, and planning how they were going to bring integrity back into journalism to make a difference by reporting the truth. They drank cheap red wine from a local vineyard, cooked fish they caught, and made love under the stars.

"You know, Marnie," said Joe, "I travel all over the world, stay at the best hotels at times, but no one makes the first cup of coffee for me like you do."

"Just the right amount of coffee in the machine, brewed for the right amount of time, with a dash of milk and one-third of a teaspoon of Manukau Honey, to sweeten it slightly; not a half, not a quarter of a teaspoon, but a third. Perfect."

They both laughed at memories of other mornings and shared coffee. "Not that I have been making many coffees for you in recent times," said Marnie wryly.

"I know," said Joe. "the last few years have been so hectic, and this one was even more so." He rubbed a hand over his face as if to wipe out the catastrophic world events he had recently reported on. Travelling to Haiti, China, weather chaos in the US and Europe. Uprisings in the Middle East. Chilian miners trapped as the world held its breath, waiting for their rescue. Ending the year with the tragic fatal explosions in Pike River Mine on the South Island of New Zealand.

The adrenaline that drove him to follow another unfolding news story was fading. He had spent years catching the first flight to wherever in the world the latest drama was unfolding; the ground imploding, another disaster to be reported, uprisings, suicide bombers, all needing him to bring the news to the world. Often Joe was the first correspondent on the scene, and his calm, measured tone as he reported the news was respected and valued around the world.

But he no longer found his job challenging. Images of another disaster, yet another war, and the suffering of innocent people, invaded his dreams and disturbed his sleep.

"Marnie I am losing heart and the stomach for this kind of life," sighed Joe. "I can't switch off anymore. The innate cruelty that people can inflict on one another, the horror of loss and death…I long to denounce the Generals, and the incompetent Government Officials who prevent aid from reaching areas of natural disasters. When I learn of the greed of smooth business men who take advantage of trusting people, conning them out of their hard earned savings, I find it hard to be impartial. And I am tired. I think it is time I hung up my Foreign Correspondent's hat."

Marnie poured more coffee, "How will you replace this hectic life you have lived for the past twenty years? After flying off to a different destination every week or so, you might find it hard to be in the same place for long."

"I don't know I'm tired I might take a sabbatical for a year, think about the next stage of my life. Maybe I'll write a book, or just write the memories for myself; it might exorcise the images behind my eyes." Joe sighed, breathed deeply, and closed his eyes turning his face to the sun now shining on the deck.

Over the years they had both had relationships; made plans for a life with other people. But they both broke off their engagements before the weddings took place. Somehow they couldn't make that final commitment. A week before Joe's marriage in New York to Rochelle, he found himself thinking more and more of Marnie and the times they'd spent together; relaxing, talking into the night, laughing over silly things. He was relieved when another crisis had blown up in the Middle East and he'd had to fly out, giving him an excuse to cancel the wedding.

Marnie had lived with Thomas in Sydney for two years. They bought a tiny house on the North Shore near the water, and were fairly happy. As time went on, Thomas wanted Marnie to give up her "'little job'" and help him build his business i.e., do all his paperwork and accounts. He was on his third business venture since she had known him. Eventually she realized - she could no longer bail Thomas out after he became bored with the routine of running a business and the hard slog needed to build it up. She saw his charm but finally walked away and was still waiting to be paid out her share of the house. Although they had both signed the mortgage, she had paid for everything. Eventually she cut her losses and flew back to New Zealand.

Joe sat up and looked at the familiar figure beside him with her green eyes and dark, pageboy-cut hair. She had a distinctive lock of hair that had turned white overnight before final exams.

He said, "Oh! Marnie, I take you for granted. You've been in my life for the past twenty odd years. I come and go, but you never protest when I disappear for months or even years. I turn up and you smile and I immediately feel better." Leaning over, he tucked the silver lock of hair behind her ear, kissed her waiting mouth, and murmured, "What would I do without you? Marry me?"

Smiling at each other, they knew that at last this was their time and they would spend the rest of their lives together. Marnie leaned on his shoulder, sighed contentedly and murmured, "Well Joe love of my life, you beat me to it – as it is a leap year I was planning to propose under the moonlight tonight." They laughed and he said, "I feel as if I have come home, and with you have hope for the future."

The Girl Who Was Found In A Sea Gull's Nest

It was Christmas Eve, and the O'Neill family had come home from the Christmas service in the village, finished dinner, and were settling round the big log fire. This would be their last Christmas together for some time, as Dominic and Liam, the two oldest sons, were leaving in the New Year to begin their new lives.

Grace and Dylan O'Neill had six tall, strong sons, all with dark hair and blue eyes; Dominic, Liam, Cormac, James, Michael, and Sam. Their seventh child was a red, haired, brown eyed daughter, ten-year old Cordelia. The extended O'Neill family had lived in the fishing village for the past four hundred years. Over the generations, many of their family had emigrated to America, England, Canada, or Australia to give their families more opportunities. But Dylan and Grace had decided to stay in Ireland. They'd renovated the big old house Dylan's great grandfather had built and settled down to raise their growing family. They had a few animals, grew what vegetables and fruit trees could survive the wild winter storms, and Dylan went out with the fishing boat that belonged to several families in the village.

They also had a secret that few people knew. But tonight the truth would be revealed and questions answered.

In the New Year Liam would be joining his Uncle Daniel's ship to begin a five-year apprenticeship as a ship's engineer. Dominic, with the encouragement and support of the local Headmaster, was joining a major newspaper in London as a very junior reporter. Both had an opportunity to build good careers, although they were sad to leave their Mam and Dad, brothers, and little sister, to say farewell to the village they had grown up in and where they had been so happy. Still, young men almost, they were excited at the prospect of a new life in front of them.

After much laughter and reminiscings, everyone grew quiet thinking of growing up in the big house on the cliff and of their happy childhood helping their father with the animals and learning to fish on the village boat. All of them grown up with a love of books and learning, encouraged by their mam, dad, and the schoolmaster at the local school.

Then Cordelia's quiet little voice broke the silence… "Dad, where did I come from?"

"Why, Cordelia, we've always told you, we found you in a seagull's nest." He laughed and the boys laughed too. The very idea….in a seagull's nest!

Then Mam said, "I think the time is right now, Dylan Cordelia has a right to know the truth, and she is old enough to understand."

"Are you sure now Grace?" replied Dylan with a concerned look.

"Yes, I'm sure, this is the right time," said Mam. The boys straightened up, no more slouching or lying on the floor. This sounded serious.

Cordelia said, "What do you mean the truth?"

"Hush now, pet, Daddy will tell you everything. Come and sit by my knee." Grace put her arm out and drew Cordelia close. Cordelia snuggled in and looked hard at her dad.

"It all began the night of the hundred year storm," said Dad.

"I remember that night," said Dominic, "the big hawthorn tree was split in two by a lightning strike."

Liam and Sam remembered how the wind had howled round the house, and how they'd been afraid the roof was going to come off. Then came the eerie, ghostly sound of the lifeboat siren howling through the storm, warning the village that a boat was in trouble.

Dylan explained that he had been one of the volunteers who had gone out in the Lifeboat to try and rescue the boat struggling in the mountainous seas and hopefully to save lives.He struggled into his wet weather gear, his big boots that could grip the wet deck, and took his torch Grace gave him a flask of tea.

"May all the Angels and Saints preserve you and bring safely home everyone on the lifeboat and those poor souls lost at sea." She hugged her husband tightly. Then she and Dominic held the door while Dylan struggled out into the storm.

"Look after your mother and brothers, Dominic," Dylan said to his oldest son.

"I will, Dad," Dominic promised.

It was a hard struggle to get down to the port where the other volunteers had made their way. John, the skipper, gave them their orders taking up their positions; the volunteers launched the Lifeboat into the treacherous stormy sea.

"The distress flares came from beyond the lighthouse. We must make our way there. Hold on tight, and keep a sharp lookout!" John shouted above the noise of the wind and crashing sea.

At times the boat seemed to tip completely perpendicular on the water as it rode the mountainous waves. It was a miracle it didn't turn over. For hours they battled up and down by the rocks under the lighthouse but they could not see any sign of a boat or survivors. Finally and reluctantly John gave the order to turn for home.

Dylan was in the prow, tied firmly with rope so he wouldn't be washed overboard. As the lifeboat turned for home, he spotted an over turned life raft from a ship that must have sunk. They continued to search and search but there was no sign of life. Reluctantly they turned for home.

As they pulled their lifeboat up to the shed, John said, "We'll clean up in the morning lads. Go home and get dried out. We'll search the shoreline for any signs of wreckage or bodies tomorrow."

Wearily the men turned for home. Dylan took the cliff path. He usually didn't come this way as it could be treacherous, but he hoped it would be quicker tonight. When he had almost reached the top of the climb he stumbled as part of the path gave way. Down he tumbled over the steep slope, stopping only when he caught a sturdy gorse bush clinging to the cliff face.

Suddenly there was silence. The wind dropped and he heard a faint mewling sound coming from where the seagulls built their nests. Thinking it might be a small animal in trouble; he rubbed the rainwater from his eyes and saw to his astonishment a small cradle fashioned like a little coracle stuck by a rock where an enormous wave must have thrown it up. He blinked again as he thought he saw a tiny hand come up. He scrambled over, grabbed the little cradle and saw a little figure like a doll strapped inside. Tucking the cradle under his arm he somehow scrambled up the cliff and ran home as fast as he could to a warm fire and Grace. She would look after this little baby.

"So you see Cordelia," said her dad softly, "when I said we found you in a seagull's nest, it was true."

Everyone was quiet, trying to imagine the night Cordelia had arrived in their family.

"I gave you your name," Dominic suddenly remembered. We were reading *"The Tempest"* at school and Cordelia was a character in it. Her name in Gaelic means "'daughter of the sea."'

"That's right," said Dad, "And we also gave you Grace as a middle name after your new mammy. You know Cordelia your mam never slept for ten days and nights while she nursed you, trying to get you to take some milk and bring your fever down. The doctor and priest didn't think you would survive."

"But you did my darling girl," said Grace. "One night I fell asleep in the rocking chair, and when I jolted awake there you were, looking up at me with those big brown eyes. Your fever was gone and you were safe."

"But do you mean you are not my real mam and dad? That my brothers are not my brothers?" Cordelia's lip trembled.

"Now, now my pet," soothed her mam, "you are truly as much our child as the boys who were born in this house."

"I read a long time ago Cordelia," said Dad, "that children chose the parents and family they are going to live with. And just as the boys chose us to be their family, so did you. Why do you think I decided to come by the cliff path that night and why did the storm suddenly still so I could hear your tiny cry? Oh! Yes my pet we are as much your family as the young people who gave you life and who we believe perished in the hundred year storm that night. Although we tramped the shoreline for weeks we never found any trace of them.""The doctor, the priest and I searched for any record of where you'd come from but there was nothing. In the end the doctor and priest decided it would be best for you to stay with the loving family who had welcomed you into their home."

Grace laughed. "Remember Dylan, the night before the storm became so fierce we were talking and laughing about those rambunctious boyos of ours and what they needed was the civilizing influence of a sister in the house."

"By the next morning we had our wish," Dylan said solemnly. "A quiet clever serene beautiful daughter to add a calming loving presence to our houseful of boys."

Cordelia's brothers all came and hugged and kissed their little sister and it seemed they all had bright eyes after hearing about the eventful start to her life.

"Liam," said Mam, "run up and fetch the big box at the back of my cupboard."

"Right, but don't tell anything more until I come down." He thundered up the stairs and was back in a moment. He put the large box down by Mam's chair.

"Open the box darlin'" Mam said, smiling at Cordelia.

Cordelia turned the lock and looked inside. Wrapped in a soft blanket was the tiny cradle shaped like a coracle. "Oh!" breathed Cordelia. "It's so small!"

"To think it—and you—survived the hundred year storm," said Dad. "It goes to show you were meant to land on the cliff by the seagull's nest, I was meant to climb up the cliff path and the storm was meant to drop so I could hear your little cry." Tears came to his eyes.

Cordelia went over and squeezed her dear dad. Then her mam and all her brothers crowded round and hugged her so tightly she knew she was the luckiest girl in the world to be surrounded by all this love and affection.

That night Cordelia had the dream she had from time to time, in which she saw a young couple the man with red gold hair like hers, the woman with brown hair and brown eyes smiling at her. This time she heard a voice. "Cordelia our darling girl, you did indeed choose your family well. We are always watching over you and love you." Then the dream faded and she never had it again.

Cordelia got up and wrapped the quilt that Mam had made around her. She sat down at the desk that Liam and Sam had made for her as a Christmas Gift, and she began to write an account of all she had heard that night. The curtains of her window were pulled back. As she looked out over the garden at the benches made by her dad and brothers from the old hawthorn she smiled remembering how they had all carved their names into the wood.

Over the wall the bright moonlight lit the cliff path, which was covered in snow that had begun to fall as they'd walked home from church. Suddenly a sea gull flew up, disturbed by a predator prowling. The bird flew across the face of the full moon, creating an image that Cordelia carried with her for the rest of her life.

Author's note: This story began when I remembered a conversation with my mum as a three year old in Ireland. "Where did I come from Mummy?" I asked.

"Why we found you in a seagull's nest" was the reply. What a great title for a story I thought a few years back. Thank you, Mum.

Coracle: *Meaning small Celtic boat made from willow rods and animal skins.*

Where Did You Get Those Eyes?

A few days after the funeral Beth let herself into the apartment and felt her beloved grandma's calm serene presence so strongly that tears fell unbidden down her face. Beth couldn't believe that she would never talk, laugh and spend time with her again.

She had promised her mother that she would go through her grandma's papers and sort out favourite paintings and treasures for family to choose before the apartment went on the market. Beth made a coffee and sat at the beautiful old desk where her grandma had loved to sit and write. She looked again at photos of her mum, aunt, uncle, and cousins, snapshots of family holidays with all of them together. Tucked behind an old-fashioned inkpot was a small, silver-framed photograph of a tall, distinguished-looking man, smiling at whoever was taking the photograph.

Suddenly Beth jumped up, knocking over her coffee; fortunately it was almost gone and didn't spill on anything important. She recognized the man in the photograph, or thought she did. Beth stood up and prowled around. Who was it? Where had she seen him before?

Then she remembered there had been a man who looked just like the figure in the picture at Grandma's funeral standing at the back of the church. As Beth and her family were walking down the aisle, he stood back and then bowed slightly as she caught his eye. His eyes were the most amazing colour grey green against tanned skin. She had felt a shiver run down her spine then went out into the sunlight and round to the graveyard for the burial.

In the apartment, Beth hurried over to the desk and picked up the photo. It couldn't be the man at the church this must be his father or uncle. Who were they? How did Grandma know them? *I wonder if Mum knows,* she thought.

Some hours later Beth had sorted papers into piles for her mum and aunt to see to, thrown out old papers that were not of interest, and emptied the drawers. And at the back of the bottom drawer she found a beautifully bound book filled with her grandma's lovely writing. Making a fresh pot of coffee, Beth sat down and began to read.

When I first arrived in India I travelled slowly, stopping at places Michael and I had planned to visit. We had spent time in the library and with travel agents, making notes for our planned trip. Ranthambore National Park, located in the Sawai Madhopur district of south Eastern Rajasthan was where I planned to spend the last two weeks of my holiday, relaxing in a beautiful comfortable, old fashioned hotel and exploring the nearby national park.

I was thoroughly enjoying my time travelling alone although it would have been wonderful if Michael had been with me. I had arrived almost two weeks earlier and was beginning to relax. When Michael died so suddenly last year, it took time for the girls and me to accept he was gone and to move on with our lives.

Beth realized this must have been an account of the trip Grandma made before her mum married and Beth was born. Fascinated, she turned again to the book.

Michael and I married young just out of university and because I became pregnant so soon with Deidre and a year later with Faith; our planned trip round the world didn't eventuate. Not that we regretted having the girls so quickly we loved being a family and watching the girls grow. Deidre was the image of her dad with his dark hair and blue eyes and Faith was like me with red hair and brown eyes. We worked hard and built a good and happy life for us. We planned that when the girls were established we would take that long overdue trip round the world.

Both girls were established in university and we were planning a trip to India. We were going to book when Michael returned from a seminar he was attending in Glasgow. He never reached home. A pileup on the motorway on a wet and rainy day left him dead and turned our lives upside down.

Beth reached for a tissue only imagining how her mum, aunt, and grandma had coped with losing their dad and husband.

A year after Michael died, I decided to take the trip we had planned. The girls were concerned about my going alone but I reassured them it was all well planned.

Peace, tranquility and calm took over all my senses as I enjoyed the comfort and pleasant fellow travelers at the hotel. Visiting the national park close by the hotel, I marveled at the diverse flora and fauna and felt they were the true treasures of India.

One week after arriving at the hotel I was enjoying a predinner drink on the wide veranda and chatting with other guests when a sudden excruciating pain struck me in the chest and I fell to the ground.

Next I knew, I was recovering consciousness drifting in and out of awareness in a hospital bed, connected to machines that measured my vital signs, wearing an oxygen mask and surrounded by medical staff. I could see a tall figure rapidly asking questions of the team around him and checking a chart. He leaned over me and said softly, "I'm Charles Grey the heart specialist. Do you still have pain?" He removed the oxygen mask told me to breathe slowly and asked if I had ever had pain like this previously.

"No, never, I've never felt pain like this in my life; I thought I was going to die." I said.

"You could have, if the hotel staff hadn't acted swiftly I think you have contracted a heart virus," replied Professor Grey.

Charles later told me what happened next. He turned gave instructions to his team and then as a tranquilizer was being given to me, he felt my hand on his sleeve. He leaned down and heard me whisper, "Where did you get those eyes?" For they were pale grey green, startling in his dark face.

He leaned close to my ear and smiled. "From my mother."

I murmured, "She must be very beautiful."

I didn't hear his soft reply, "She was."

Then I went into cardiac arrest.

I was told it was three days later when I became aware of a dim room and the quiet murmur of voices around me.

Someone said, "She is very lucky to be alive I can't believe she survived."

"I've never seen the professor work so long on a patient. He usually accepts when it is too late, but really, I believe he brought her back from the dead," said another voice.

"Oh! Look! Sleeping Beauty is stirring. How do you feel Geraldine?" asked the ward sister.

I replied, "A bit dopey, but what on earth happened? Last thing I remember, besides bits of being in hospital is enjoying a quiet drink on the veranda of the hotel, and then I felt this horrendous pain."

"Professor Grey has been to check on you. He is very pleased with your progress. He is at a fundraising dinner tonight but will call in on his way home. If you are still awake he will explain everything. Now try and rest. Your results are looking good," answered the sister.

I stretched my limbs checking for any discomfort. Nothing, no pain in my chest so I dozed, thanking God I was alive.

Later that night, when the ward was quiet and the lights dimmed, I could see the ward sister sitting at her desk talking quietly to the nurses who came and went. A figure appeared at the door of my room and came over to my bed. His shirt was startlingly white in the dim light and an untied bow tie dangled from his collar.

"Ah, I see you have rejoined us in the land of the living." Charles Grey sat on the side of my bed and took my hand. My pulse unaccountably began to race.

"How are you feeling?" he asked.

"What happened? I never had heart problems before."

"It looks like a virus caused inflammation and then a heart attack. It was one of the most unusual cases I have seen. Very interesting from a clinical point of view." He raised his eyebrows and smiled.

I took his hand, tears rolling down my face. "I don't know how to thank you. You saved my life."

Professor Grey gently brushed my tears away. "Well I think I had to save you. There are many other things for you to achieve in life. Besides no one else has ever complimented me on my eyes as she was dying. When we'd tried everything else I held your heart in my hands and willed it to start beating again." He smiled. "It worked!"

For several hours we sat and talked about our lives. He had two almost grown sons and a socialite wife who spent most of her time in Europe attending fashionable parties. Occasionally she flitted home unsettling everyone and then flying back to the next yacht party.

He talked about his work and his determination to improve health care for heart patients. He told me about his mother part French part English who had died of a heart attack when he was only twelve because there were no facilities to save her. He'd gone to live *with his grandparents, an irascible old retired British army colonel and his beautiful Indian wife. Charles's father had died before he was born, climbing in the Swiss Alps. He and Charles's mother Celine had met while students at the Sorbonne.*

I told him of my life with Michael and our daughters, and how Michael had died last year just as we were planning this trip. I talked of Deidre's and Faith's ambitions for the future and my job helping young impoverished mothers to care first for themselves and then their families. I described my love of painting and of rare and beautiful plants. We both tried to convey to each other a lifetime of living before fate had brought us together.

The next day the ward sister told me she had come into the room the night before and stopped. There seemed to be something extraordinary between the two people and in the quiet murmur of their voices which didn't bear interrupting. She quietly turned and left.

I'd felt it too. The doctor and his patient, who had met only three days earlier and spoken for just a few hours, knew there was a connection between them that would never be broken. They also knew they would never meet again.

Reluctantly he said at last, "You must get some rest I have contacted the heart specialist in your home town and the airline you are travelling with. You will be well enough to travel in a few days and will be well cared for on the journey home. Contact David Nicholson at this hospital on your return I have sent him all my notes and he will keep an eye on you. We studied together he is a good man. Unfortunately I am flying to Geneva tomorrow morning; I must go as I am the principal speaker, so I shan't see you again."

He paused "You and my mother are the only women in my life who have touched my heart, and I shall carry yours with me always."

Impulsively I said "Wait just a moment," I took out my small camera "I want to remember always this time of my life."

Charles picked up my left hand turned it over and kissed the palm. I took the photograph. "Safe journey," he said. Then he turned and walked out of the room and my life.

"And to you," I whispered. "For all of your life, safe journey."

Beth sat with tears running down her face. Then she suddenly remembered when Grandma was dying and they were all sitting with her how she had suddenly opened her eyes, looked over Beth's shoulder towards the door and said clearly, "Where did you get those eyes?" Then she had smiled closed her eyes and drifted away. Now Beth understood what she had said.

Beth didn't know it, but at the same time her grandmother was dying thousands of miles away, an eminent heart surgeon was also leaving the world his sons and grandsons by his bed. Early one morning he opened his eyes smiled as if he recognized someone and said clearly "Safe journey." Then closed his eyes and was gone.

Beth looked again at the little photo and could see that the smiling man had been holding the photographer's hand. Her grandma's hand.

Beth couldn't wait to tell her mother about what she had found. As she picked up the phone to call her, the intercom buzzed. "That must be Mum now," she said and buzzed the door release. She went and opened a bottle of wine—they'd need it when Beth told her what she'd discovered.

A knock sounded at the door. She opened it smiling, and said, "I unlocked it for you Mum." Then she staggered back. Standing on the doorstep was the man in the photograph. But no, it couldn't be he was too young.

"Who, who are you? What do you want? Sorry, sorry I've just had a shock."

He put a hand out to steady her. "I apologize for the intrusion. My name is Charles Grey."

Beth interrupted him. "Did I see you at my grandma's funeral?"

"Yes you did. You see my grandfather died recently and I believe he knew and perhaps was in love with your grandmother. I found a diary he wrote and I felt compelled to find the woman he'd thought about every day since he'd met her, only to find when I arrived in England that she had died the same day he did."

Beth opened the door wider and invited in the grandson of the man who had not only saved her grandma's life but had captured her heart as well. It was extraordinary, unbelievable that such love could endure.

He stretched out his hand, and as they clasped hands both felt a jolt of recognition. Maybe fate had decided they were going to have the relationship that their grandparents had been denied.

Paros

1 September 1975

Dear Charles,

I will arrive at the train station at six fifteen tomorrow evening. Don't worry about meeting me. I will take a taxi.

I have contacted the Croeso Boutique Hotel on the Greek island of Paros where I have spent several restoring visits in the past. The innkeepers, Stefan and Ana have accommodation available for you and will collect you from the ferry when it arrives on Thursday. The air travel is booked with an open ticket and a car will meet you at the airport to take you to the ferry. There will be plenty of time to catch it just in case the flight is delayed.

Charles, I believe this is an opportunity for you to get away to try and recover from the tragic events of the last year. I am still trying to get my head around it myself and can only imagine how it has affected you.

I will pack your bags. You know how I love packing and organizing people. I'll drive you to the airport Wednesday morning and then arrange with Mrs. Banks next door to keep an eye on things while you are away.

I am not giving you the chance to refuse, that is why I am "'railroading' "you. I know it will take more than a holiday to erase from your mind what has happened but I know that Paros will bring some peace to your soul.

With fond love

Lavinia

Robyn P. Murray

21 September 1975

Dear Lavinia,

Thank you for arranging my stay here on the beautiful island of Paros. The Croeso Boutique Hotel is everything you promised. This evening I am sitting on the terrace with a chilled bottle of wine, dishes of olives, cheese and bread, breathing the wonderful air and absorbing the light, inhaling the smell of lemon, wild thyme and pine. A blazing sun setting below the horizon has turned the Aegean Sea scarlet and gold and somehow I feel protected, safe, my head not turning over the accident that robbed me of my family and almost my sanity. At times it feels the accident happened only yesterday but I know that it's been almost six months since that bleak chance of fate and being in the wrong place at the wrong time.

Did you know that the couple who run the hotel originally came here from Wales over twenty years ago? They renovated an old farmhouse to make it a bed and breakfast but within a few years they never had to advertise, word of mouth meant they were always full. A few years later they extended to build the lovely place it is today. Did you know that the name of the hotel, Croeso, is Welsh for welcome?

My nervous system is slowly unclenching, and I am seduced by the location, and by my hosts calm acceptance that I am here to renew my spirit and do not always want to engage in conversation. Other guests are an interesting mixture of people from around the world. One elderly lady from Yorkshire has spent three months of each year here for the last seven years. At dinner, a few nights ago, we were the only guests dining in the hotel and she quietly asked if I minded our having dinner together. How could I refuse a Miss Marple lookalike? At the end of the evening, I am not sure how, she had uncovered the whole sorry tale of the past six months by making observations and not exactly asking questions. She didn't issue platitudes or the usual comments about the healing power of time. I felt comforted if that is the correct word. I, such a private person, have never revealed so much of myself to someone I didn't know. I think she should have been recruited by MI6 as an interrogator she certainly could have given George Smiley a run for his money. I slept through the night for the first time in six months.

I have established a pattern for my days. I take an early morning walk down the hillside to swim in the turquoise sea. After breakfast comes a walk and some exploring, perhaps some reading or writing in the afternoon, and then I join my hosts and other guests for dinner if I feel strong enough.

At dawn on the first morning after my arrival, I found myself swimming out towards the horizon; it seemed an easy escape, a way to drift into oblivion. Then I looked back over my shoulder at the shore. The sun was just painting the beach and edge of the water rosy pink and water kicked up by my feet sparkled like precious jewels in the crisp morning air. Something changed and I wasn't yet ready to leave this often unexpectedly beautiful world.

Lavinia, my dear sister, I thank you as always for your support over the years, particularly during this bleak time in my life. I am slowly recovering and you have strengthened me.

Last evening while flicking through old visitors books, I saw an entry by a Lavinia Buchanan and a George Harrison. That wasn't you by any chance, the summer you went missing?

Blessings,
Charles

30 September 1975
Dear Charles,

How good to hear from you and that you are gradually finding some peace in the secluded retreat that is Paros.

How observant you are! Yes, that was my signature. It was a magical summer for me when I "dropped out of life" for a few months. George and I laughed and lived each day without thought of the future and what lay ahead. Both of us needed time out from the pressures of people and life, and it set us firmly on the successful paths of our individual success. Not together, but we were there for each other in the right place at the right time.

Now tell me Charles, have you been writing? If you can without putting pressure on yourself I feel it will help.

Give my very kind regards to Stefan and Ana. They helped restore my faith in humankind and I hope they have done the same for you.

Let me know when you are ready to come back and I will arrange with Mrs. Banks to get things ready for you.

Take care I think of you often

With love,

Lavinia

10 October, 1975

Dear Lavinia,

I feel I am ready to face the world again. I have booked my ticket to arrive at Heathrow Monday week at twelve noon.

I would like to take advantage of your penchant for organizing things and ask you to arrange with the funeral director to collect the bodies of Susanna, Phillip, and Adriana from the mortuary where they are being held; and to fix a time for a funeral service at St Cuthbert's in Carter Road for the following Friday.

I know that people found it strange I didn't have the funeral after the accident but I couldn't face it. I thought I would lose my mind. Now I feel strong enough to give them the funeral they deserve and to decide what I want to do with the rest of my life without them. They will always be with me, birthdays, anniversaries, Christmas. They made their individual mark on the world in their own way, and I will carry them in my heart all of my life.

Again Lavinia I must thank you for being so strong and helping me during this survival part of my journey to finally face what happened and to honour their memory by continuing to live.

With love

Charles

The Well-Travelled Suitcase

So this is where I end my long life, waiting for a truck to take me to the dump. The elderly suitcase sighed. As the morning sun rose over the hills surrounding the quiet suburban village, the suitcase settled more comfortably against the tree where she had been dumped along with the rest of unwanted rubbish.

She dreamed of how her life had begun in Paris in a fashionable shop on the Champs Élysées as the latest Louis Vuitton design. Placed in the centre of the beautiful window display, she'd waited for someone to come along and buy her so she could begin a fabulous life of travel.

Forty minutes after the suitcase was placed in the window, a long car drew up outside the shop. Out stepped the beautiful Princess Marie Chantal Louise and her godmother, the Grand Duchess from a small but very wealthy Principality. They were staying in Paris while they prepared for an eagerly awaited trip to New York.

An hour later, after drinking a glass of champagne and choosing the latest trunks and suitcases, including the little case in the window, the ladies swept out to go back to their hotel and oversee their maids packing for them.

From that day on, the beautiful handcrafted case travelled to many different destinations, though never far from her owner's possession. She was always being either being packed or unpacked by the Princess's personal maid, Josie. When not in use, the case was covered by a soft cloth and stored carefully to protect her beautiful cover.

After years of care and attention, travel and being admired, suddenly it all came to an end. Princess Marie Chantal eloped with her mother's butler, and the little case was left behind. Josie, who had always loved the case, received it as a going away present when she left the household to take up a position as a junior typist with a major newspaper in London. She had been given a reference and introduction to the editor by the Grand Duchess's brother, who owned part of the newspaper.

In the evenings, Josie began to write her account of life as a Ladies maid with aristocratic families. She stored her writing in the beautiful little Louis Vuitton case.

Several years later, Josie fell madly in love with one of the subeditors at the paper. He proposed and her writing was put to one side, if not forgotten. She and Stuart were busy planning a low key wedding, and packing to emigrate to Melbourne, leaving behind the turmoil that was Europe. They would begin a new life, sailing shortly after their marriage.

The Louis Vuitton case was hastily wrapped and packed in a tea chest with other larger items, and just before embarkation was sent to the ship to be stored in the hold until they arrived in Melbourne.

So began a very different life in Australia, building a life with Stuart and Josie's growing family. From time to time over the years, Josie took out the little case, gazed at the contents, added some more notes, and sighed over memories of her time spent as a young personal maid to the Princess, witnessing the intrigues, glamorous parties, affairs. She found it difficult to believe that had been part of her world when she was much younger. Josie thought about writing that novel she had planned before she'd met Stuart, but then life and her family took priority and the idea was shelved once again. Eventually the case was relegated to the loft and forgotten.

Decades later, after Josie's funeral, the family returned home to find the house ransacked. Whoever had broken in had even gone into the loft and taken all that might be worth anything. The police said that a well-organized gang had been operating throughout the state and was thought to be from New Zealand.

A few weeks later, in a quiet suburb on the outskirts of Auckland, a large shipping container with the proceeds of countless burglaries carried out in Victoria, Australia, was unpacked. Coming across the old rather dusty case the gang leader gave a cursory glance inside and then tossed it aside to be thrown out for the rubbish collection next day.

Early the next morning, Jim, who raised funds for a local charity, was driving down the streets where the unwanted items were put out for the annual inorganic collection. He sometimes picked up things that could bring in a few dollars and then put the money to good use. Jim saw the little case almost buried under other rubbish and leaves from the tree above. He drew in his breath; it looked a bit like the photograph of an early Louis Vuitton case that he and his girlfriend, Marie, had been looking at in an old 1930s magazine over the weekend. Could it possibly be Louis Vuitton? Jim stopped picked up the little case, dusted off rubbish and leaves, and placed it carefully in the back of his van.

Marie loved vintage items and collected at weekend markets when she could. She worked in the local library and belonged to a writer's group, and her stories reflected the era that fascinated her. The 1920s and '30s. After dinner that night, Jim said, "I think I have a surprise for you." He cleared the table and placed the little case on a piece of newspaper. "I thought I recognized this when I was doing my rounds this morning it was thrown out for rubbish collection. What do you think? Is it like the photos in the magazine we were looking at over the weekend?"

A gasp of delight from Marie confirmed his guess was right. "I don't believe it; early Louis Vuitton! It's beautiful. Jim, you are a genius!" She flung her arms round his neck and kissed him. "I wonder where it came from."

Opening the case, Marie stroked the beautiful lining, which was a little the worse for wear, having been somewhere damp. She felt something behind the silk and carefully felt for an opening. She drew out an envelope and then three more. Jim and Marie sat for a moment gazing at the four bulky envelopes, which were packed with sheets of lined paper filled with writing in fading ink. "This looks like a long evening ahead of reading. I'll make a pot of tea," said Jim.

Marie was already looking at dates to see where to begin. It was early morning before Jim and Marie finished reading the incredible stories written almost a century ago.

A year later, Marie's bestseller, *The Well-Travelled Suitcase*, was published. Josie's well documented insight into life with the Princess and the people who surrounded her was perfect material for the novel Marie had always dreamed of writing. Marie and Jim had talked with legal publishing experts to ensure that there would not be any problem with plagiarism, but it was accepted that the notes had been written over seventy years earlier, so all was well and safe for Marie to adapt the stories for her novel.

In the front of the book, Marie acknowledged Josie and hoped she would have been happy that the notes she made of her life and experiences were being avidly read and enjoyed. The public's timeless interest in programmes like *Upstairs Downstairs* and *Downton Abbey* meant the book was already in its third printing and there was talk of a television series.

When Marie was on a world tour promoting her book, she was invited to the Louis Vuitton head office in Paris, where they restored the little case to its former glory. They wanted to buy the case back, but Marie refused; the case meant so much to her, and it was a connection to Josie. The beautiful boutique made do with a photograph of Marie with the case and a copy of her book.

Jim and Marie bought a lovely home with the proceeds of sales from *The Well-Travelled Suitcase*. The little case itself, which had been picked up from rubbish on a leafy suburban street, was given pride of place in the study on a small 1930s table. Marie was working on a sequel, and her agent was in discussions with Hollywood about the possibility of a movie.

Morning Rounds: Mrs. Jones

The doors to Ward 7 opened and in bustled doctors, students and attendant medical staff to carry out morning rounds for the trauma patients. It had been another busy night in the large city hospital, and as well as Accident and Emergency coping with the usual round of stupid accidents, there had been a multi-vehicle motorway crash and a major fire in a nearby apartment block. As more and more patients arrived, new patients were placed on trolleys as they came in and lined up in the hallways. All the hospitals in the city were overcrowded with the emergencies.

Ward 7's postoperative wing was full to overflowing. The junior registrars, doctors, and nurses had been working fifteen-hour shifts, running on adrenaline; unsure when they would be relieved, and trying very hard to keep alert.

Halfway down the ward, the medical staff came to a bed where a woman lay with a drip in one hand while the other hand plucked restlessly at the sheet. Picking up the chart clipped at the end of the bed, Dr. Maxwell said, "Good morning, Mrs. Jones."

"Morning" came the shaky reply.

"About time you lot came to check on us," said a voice from the next bed.

"We'll be with you in a moment. We are just seeing Mrs. Jones," said the staff nurse.

"I'm Mrs. Jones," said both women in unison.

Swiftly one of the medical staff picked up the chart from the next bed. "Are you Mrs. Tessa Jones?"

"Yep, that's me," came the answer from the first bed.

"No, that's my name" was the reply from the next bed.

Silence hung over the group, and then they went into a huddle and scrutinized both charts. What were the chances of there being two Mrs. Tessa Jones, both forty-eight, both admitted after the motorway crash? Both had bandaged heads, both had arms in slings.

Screens were quickly drawn round the beds and a nurse dispatched to find the administrator and manager of the hospital. Trying not to alarm both women, the staff went over their medical information again. One woman had been in a car that had been tailgated by a bus; the other had been a passenger on the bus. One had multiple fractures, the other a ruptured spleen, injuries to her head, and a broken arm. Both had been unconscious and covered in blood. Details of both women had been taken from their handbags, which had been placed in the ambulance that took them to hospital after they were pulled from the wreckage around them. Staff had tried to contact their next of kin, but as yet no one had come forward. The handbags must have been mixed up.

While a student nurse stayed with each woman, reassuring them, asking for more details, and taking vital signs, senior consultants and administrative staff tried to sort out what had happened amid the chaos in A & E the previous night. It looked like the wrong Mrs. Jones had had her spleen removed.

Each woman was taken into a private room and rechecked from top to toe. Never had a more thorough medical check been carried out. Mrs. Tessa Jones #1, (who was two months older, turned out to have a heart murmur. Mrs. Tessa Jones #2 had a raging chest infection. The medical misadventure was hastily corrected; the correct spleen removed, and exhausted staff admonished for the mistakes.

The two Mrs. Joneses ended up in a small ward together, recovering and enjoying the unexpected extra attention. They lay back and replied weakly to enquiries about how they were feeling. "I'm a little better, thank you, but I could just manage another cup of tea and a piece of cake."

On their own the two Mrs. Tessa Jones formed a firm friendship.

"They have stuffed up somewhere along the way and are trying to cover it up," the older Mrs. Jones said. "But I reckon we'll take everything that is due to us, we deserve it."

"I suspect you're right Tess old girl," said the other Mrs. Jones. "Make them sweat a bit. Still at least they didn't take the wrong leg off." And the two new friends went into hoots of laughter and dunked another biscuit into their satisfyingly strong cups of tea.

Facing up to the media when they were discharged from hospital and questioned if they were going to sue the hospital for the mix up in their treatment. The two Mrs Jones paused then looked at each other and smiled. Each one speaking in turn they said "'they appreciated the treatment they had received from the hospital after the mistake had been discovered, and all the staff work very hard so what good would it do suing them? What's more they had each made a good friend, they were alive so all in all they felt very lucky.'"

The two Mrs Jones left the hospital in a taxi provided by the administrator and waiting at home were huge baskets of food and treats, Mrs Jones the younger received a new television and Mrs Jones the elder a new washing machine. Life was looking up they said as they had another cup of tea.

Banana Split

They sat in anxious silence, carefully watching every move Mr. Johnston made. The four children had been working hard all morning, and now was the moment they had all been waiting for.

During the summer holidays they had rattled around the town, gone out to Judy's uncle's farm, played ball, waded in the river, and generally had the time of their ten-year-old lives. Now they needed some money. *E.T. the Extra-Terrestrial* was showing at the local picture house and they desperately wanted to see the movie. No one had any cash, and pocket money wasn't part of their young lives.

Bill, the ideas man of the gang had suggested they smarten themselves up and visit the owner of the local milk bar Mr. Johnston, to see if he had any jobs that needed doing. Bill went in first as he had the confidence to talk with grown-ups.

"Morning, Mr. Johnston," said the bright faced young Bill.

"Good morning to you too son," said Mr. Johnston with a smile. "What can I do for you?"

"Well sir, it is really more what I can do for you." answered Bill earnestly. "My name is Bill, and you see, me and my friends want to earn some money for a special project we work hard and don't charge much." He screwed his face up anxiously waiting for Mr. Johnston's answer.

Mr. Johnston hid a smile. "Well as it happens, my assistant can't come in today and I do need the storeroom cleared out and tidied. Are you sure you and your young friends are strong enough to work hard for four hours without stopping?"

"Oh! yes sir!" Bill beamed. "We are reliable, hard workers and I am sure you will be satisfied with the job we do." Already he could see them all sitting in a row in the picture house, watching *E.T.*

"Bring your colleagues in and we will discuss terms," said Mr. Johnson.

Bill swaggered a little as he went outside. "We got the job," he said proudly. "Now we have to go in and discuss terms."

Three jaws dropped at the words "'discuss terms,'" but their backs straightened a little. They followed Bill inside.

Mr. Johnston eyed the four anxious little faces in front of him. "Mmm. Do you think you are reliable and strong enough to work steadily for four hours and do a good job?"

"Oh! yes sir!" chorused the four skinny little figures in front of him.

"If you do a good job and carry out all the tasks on my list, then you will get four dollars each. That is one dollar per hour. How does that sound?'

Three young mouths opened to say "yes, that is great," but Bill interrupted. "Aw! Mr. Johnston it's hard work in the heat. We would need a drink. Could you add a soda to our pay?" Bill bit his lip and, twisted his hands behind his back, wondering if he had gone too far.

But Mr. Johnston smiled and said, "I will come in after two hours and if you are doing a good job, you can have a ten-minutes break and a soda each."

Four delighted faces beamed up at him. The children quickly followed Mr. Johnston into the storeroom behind the soda parlour and he showed them where the boxes needed to be stacked for taking away, and where to find the big brooms for sweeping up the sidewalk. There were also shelves to be restocked and other boxes to be unpacked.

Mr. Johnston went back into the store when the bell rang, letting him know another customer wanted attention. Quietly keeping an eye on the children over the morning, he was impressed with Bill's skill at organizing the others.

Two hours passed and the storeroom was beginning to resemble the neat place he liked it to be. Mr. Johnston went in with a tray holding four large glasses filled with cream soda, a scoop of ice cream, a long straw and spoon. Four dirty faces looked up at him gratefully. Silence reigned as the sodas were devoured.

"You're all doing a good job," said Mr. Johnston. "I am very pleased so far. Carry on and in two hours I will see you with your pay." He took the glasses and spoons back; licked almost clean.

"Oh!" sighed Judy, "that was the best thing I've ever tasted."

"Come on, let's finish the job," Bill said firmly. "And when we collect our pay let me do the talking I have an idea."

By the time midday arrived Mr. Johnston stood with his hands on his hips and surveyed the storeroom. The shelves were stacked, and everything was neat, tidy, and swept clean. "Well I have to admit I didn't think you kids would do such a bang up job. Let's go to the store and I'll get your pay."

"Thank you Mr. Johnston." said Bill. "But can I ask you something?"

"Sure Bill," answered Mr. Johnston wondering what this smart youngster was going to come out with.

"Well as we do a good job, I was thinking we might ask around for other jobs" Bill stuttered a little. "I - I was wondering if you would recommend us."

"Sure I will. I am very pleased with what you have done, and if I ever need some help again, I will be glad to ask you and your team." Mr. Johnston smiled at the four tired, dirty young people.

"One more thing, Mr. Johnston," said Bill pointing to a picture over the counter. "How much does that cost?"

"Why, that's a Super Dooper Dish, Bill. It costs four dollars."

Bill went into a huddle with his friends then faced Mr. Johnston again. "Could we please have one dish and four spoons, and then you pay us three dollars each?"

They sat anxiously on stools, carefully watching every move the storekeeper made. They saw the most enormous banana split grow in front of them, with chocolate sauce, whipped cream, ice cream, and four cherries on top.

Sitting at a table with their long spoons, each of them took a turn eating a spoonful and enjoying the most delicious banana split they had ever tasted. Slowly the confection disappeared, every mouthful savoured until the plate was clean and shiny. Wow! What a day! A job done well, good pay, and two delicious treats; then tomorrow the picture house and *E.T.* What a wonderful end to the summer holidays.

Twenty years later Bill and his friends, who had gone their separate ways after school but still kept in touch, met at Mr. Johnston's funeral. They remembered the day they had earned their first pay and, learned some good lessons, and how nothing had ever compared to the taste of that banana split.

The Twig

"Is it a big tree, Nan?" Mickey looked at his grandmother in a puzzled fashion.

Kathleen was looking after her grandson, while her son, Joe and daughter-in-law, Anya, were at Starship Hospital with their little daughter Bridie. The doctor who had suspected meningitis sent them off early that morning. To distract Mickey and herself, Kathleen had suggested they go up to the attic and look at the family tree. It was in a big sea chest that had belonged to her grandfather, a sea captain, and it had amused her, her brothers and sisters, and her children over the years. It was full of maps, family photographs, treasures belonging to past generations, and the wonderful huge chart of the family tree.

"No, Mickey, it isn't a tree that grows in the garden but a family tree which shows all the family down the years, grandpa's, grandma's, uncles, aunts, cousins, your mam and dad—and it grows every time another member of the family is born."

They climbed the stairs to the room packed with a lifetime of memories, at the back was the big wooden chest. Kathleen lifted the lid and took a box carefully out of the chest. *"Maybe it will stop me worrying about the baby,"* She said to herself.

Five minutes later they were seated at the big dining room table, and Kathleen carefully took out the thick sheets of paper carefully begun by Great Uncle Paddy all those many years ago. Every generation there was always one family member who took on the job of adding the marriages, deaths, and births of the growing family on the chart.

Mickey had good concentration for a seven year old and waited patiently for his nana to tell him about the family tree. He was secretly pleased it wasn't a real tree; it might have broken the roof if it had grown too big. He had a vivid imagination.

Kathleen carefully unfolded the papers, putting them in the correct order. "Look, Mickey. Right at the top is your great, great, great grandpa James and grandma Margaret Dinsmore, who were born in Ireland but came out to New Zealand 150 years ago."

They looked at each branch, and then Kathleen said, "Now then, see that new branch, Mickey? There is your mam and your daddy, and underneath is your name, Michael Joseph Dinsmore, and the date you were born. Beside you is little Bridget Mary Dinsmore and her date of birth."

"All those branches, Nan…" said Mickey…Does that make me a twig, and Bridie will be a twiglet?" He whooped with a seven year old boy's humour.

Kathleen swooped him up in her arms…"Ah! Michael Og, you're a delight." Her heart lifted with love for her grandson.

"What's an Og, Nana?" he asked, attention fastening on the unfamiliar word.

"It's an Irish word meaning 'little.' A daddy might be called Michael and his son Michael Og so people would know who they were talking about. But mostly it is a term of affection, my Mickey Og."

Mickey looked at the chart again and suddenly asked, "Why are we at the top of the tree again Nana?"

"You can't be," said Kathleen. "It must be a mistake." Putting on her glasses she saw very faintly a tiny branch with small script. Her heart gave a lurch. Why had she never seen it before when she looked at it, first with her grandmother and, parents and then her children?

"Michael Joseph Dinsmore, age seven, died as a result of a tragic accident, and Bridget Mary Dinsmore, eighteen months, died of diphtheria," it read, and bore today's date eighty years earlier. The ghosts of dozens of Irish ancestors walked over Kathleen's grave. She shivered and folded up the papers carefully.

"Let's have a cup of tea and go for a walk in Cornwall Park, Mickey, now the rain has stopped," said Kathleen, trying to distract Mickey and herself from the coincidence of the dates of the deaths of two children, with the same names of her beloved grandchildren.

"Yeah! Let's go," said Mickey. "We can have a swing, collect cones, and see the sheep." He was always a busy boy. They wrapped up warmly. Although it was now sunny, there was a cold wind. But Cornwall Park was always a delight no matter the weather.

Together they walked through the park, patting dogs and, marvelling at the trees with old autumn leaves on one side and burgeoning pink blossoms on the other, thanks to a few days of sunny weather. Running after Mickey, Kathleen began to feel better. Out in the crisp fresh air, she put out of her mind that several generations ago, two small children with the same names of her grandchildren had died on today's date. Ignoring the chill on her neck, she pointed out a playful dog to her grandson.

They came out of the trees and headed up the road to the old house and the kiosk to buy an ice cream. No matter what the weather, Mickey always loved ice cream. He danced ahead, waving a stick like a sword at an imaginary lion and shouting that it was going to eat Kathleen. Suddenly he saw a small dog sitting on the other side of the road and turned to run towards it.

Kathleen felt a roaring in her head. The background changed; the trees were younger, smaller, the road was rocky and unpaved. The car that was bearing down on them was a vintage model. She tried to run but was hampered by her clothes—she no longer wore jeans, but her legs were encased in a long tweed skirt, and she wore a long, restricting coat and a hat pulled down over her face. What was happening? Everything was in slow motion and seemed a long way away. All at once she heard herself yell, "no, no, not again!" and threw herself forwards. Her legs, covered in jeans once more, reached Michael. She scooped him up in her arms and fell in the gutter on the other side of the road, dazed but holding tight to her grandson.

"Oh! Sorry! Sorry," gasped a young girl dressed in twenties-style clothes. Her car was indeed a vintage model. It occurred to Kathleen that she must be on her way to the vintage rally in town that day. The girl jumped down from the high front seat, while her white-faced passengers remained in the back seat.

"Yes, yes, we're fine, just a bit shaken. Nothing an ice cream won't fix," said Kathleen reassuringly. She wanted them gone, to think over what had happened and calm her thudding heart.

"Please, Nana, you're squeezing me," said Mickey in a muffled voice.

"Oh! Sorry, my pet, I got such a fright. Are you OK?" She peered anxiously into her darling grandson's face.

"Yes, I'm alright. Sorry Nan, I shouldn't have run on the road."

"No, Michael Dinsmore, that is not what you do. You've taken years off my life. What would I have told your poor mam and dad? Promise me you will always look before crossing a road, and only go when it is safe." She gave him another hug.

"I will, Nana, I'm sorry."

"Well, then, I think we can treat ourselves to a Rush Munro's ice cream, don't you think?" His nana smiled.

"Yes, please, Nana Og." Mickey grinned. "Og is a word of affection, Nan." He hurried up to check out the ice cream flavours.

Seated on the warm stone steps across from the restaurant and old house, Kathleen with her lemon and gin ice cream and Mickey with his double chocolate, they looked down at the trees and people walking and the beautiful park, and each went over their own thoughts.

Was that how young Michael from eighty years ago had died, Kathleen wondered? Was he run over by a car? while his grandmother, with her long, heavy clothes, was unable to reach him in time? She wondered who would believe her if she tried to tell them. Was it a coincidence, or had Kathleen's young Mickey been saved by his great great grandmother, who had been unable to save her own young Michael? Whatever had happened, thank God for coincidence, physic insight, family trees, and jeans! But what about Bridie?

A familiar roaring filled Kathleen's ears. This time she was looking down on a little iron cot. Two weeping young people and a doctor in old fashioned clothes, looked down on the dead baby. Again Kathleen found her voice and shouted. "No!! No!" Then the picture changed, and the ward where little Bridie had been admitted came into focus. Anya and Joe were smiling and looking at the doctor, who was holding a solemn but wide awake Bridie. Everything was all right. Thank God!

"You're squeezing me again, nana. What's wrong?" asked Mickey.

"Not a thing, my pet, everything is wonderful. Why don't we go up and see Bridie in hospital? I am sure she is better, I have a feeling everything is going to be grand."

As Kathleen fastened Mickey into his car seat, he showed her a little twig with leaves from the past season on one side and a few pink blossoms for the new season on the other. "A present for the little twiglet," he said, smiling.

"Good boy, what a lovely idea." Kathleen shut the car door and they drove to the hospital. She thought she had better write an account of this day and put it with the family tree papers. Maybe when Mickey was grown and had a family of his own, he would remember.

Twenty five years later two weeks after Kathleen's funeral, and one week after his baby daughter was born, Michael opened an envelope that his beloved nana had left for him. Inside was a dried little twig wrapped in acid free tissue paper. It was the twig he had picked for his little sister when the family brought Bridie home from Starship Children's Hospital. Along with it was a letter Kathleen had written twenty-five years earlier.

He read the letter twice and checked the date before dropping the paper with his grandmother's familiar handwriting on the table. He thought of that day in the park all those years ago. He remembered in sharp detail the events of the day. Finding the faint record of two children with the same names as his sister and himself. The identical dates. The family tree. Different types of trees in the park with leaves from the past season and new blossoms for the future. Sitting in the gutter, with Nana holding him tightly. The taste of chocolate ice cream.

"I don't believe it," he muttered.

Believe it. Kathleen's voice sounded in his head. *You and Bridie are still here with your own families now.*

Another little Kathleen Ann Dinsmore. He smiled at a photograph of his nana holding his hand. They were smiling at each other at some long forgotten joke.

"Watch over your namesake; Nana Og," Michael said. "And thank you for giving me my life and allowing me to add my children's names to the family tree."

The Unfinished Dance

Poppy was about to shut up the vintage shop she was managing for her cousin Clare when a truck with a builder's logo on the side drew up, brakes screeching. The driver, a tall, tanned, fair haired young man, jumped out, easily picked up an old trunk from the back of the truck, shouldered the door open, and came into the shop.

"I'm not too late, am I?" He grinned and put the trunk on the ground. "I'm renovating an old house on the outskirts of town. Found this in the attic and thought of your shop. The new owners told me to burn any rubbish, but I remembered my sister got a great dress here for a party and thought you might like the clothes. I think they are from the 1920's."

"Fabulous," said Poppy, smiling back at him. His grin was infectious. "That's very kind. Can I pay you something for them?"

He laughed. "No thanks, I just feel they are too interesting to be burned and deserve another party or two. I think there is some history there." He rushed out of the shop, jumped in his truck, and roared off with a wave.

Poppy locked up, pulled down the blinds, and spent the next few hours entranced with the contents of the trunk. They had been beautifully wrapped and somehow survived all the years of being locked away without fading or disintegrating. She came across some clothes that appeared to have watermarks on them, though. Suddenly Poppy felt the clothes had been packed away by someone who was crying. She sat back on her heels and wondered why the clothes had been packed away and forgotten. Most of them looked fairly unworn.

At the very bottom of the trunk lay an old fashioned gramophone complete with horn. Separately packed and wrapped in fine, bright, beautiful silk scarves was a pile of old records. Poppy unpacked them carefully, wound up the gramophone, and put on a record. The shop filled with the joyous sound of the Charleston. It was infectious music and she couldn't help swaying in time as she went into the tiny kitchen at the back to put the kettle on and make some tea.

Poppy smiled as she thought of the beautiful flapper dresses and, long strings of beads. Headbands, feathers, and tiny bags on chains. Men's evening suits with tails. Wonderful shirts, some slightly yellowed with age. Bow ties. Fantastic shoes with straps and heels for dancing the night away.

As the music wound down. Poppy became aware of laughter and voices in the shop! She went through and saw that some of the clothes hangers were empty, and two ethereal young people were jitterbugging in time to the music.

"Oh! Wind it up again darling. We haven't finished dancing, and we can't hold the handle!' A young blonde girl waved her ghostly hand at Poppy to show her she could see through it.

"Who who are you?" Poppy stuttered, wondering how on earth anyone could have gotten through the double locked door of the shop. Somehow she wasn't afraid of these young people, though she realized they must be ghosts—as she could clearly see through them to the shop walls.

"This is Jack and I'm Primrose. Thank you for unpacking our clothes. We have been earthbound for nearly ninety years. Jack asked me to marry him at the last of the summer balls, and we were planning to tell our families and friends after we had finished dancing the night away."

Jack continued, "Sadly, Monty waved his arms too energetically and knocked the candelabra over. The curtains caught fire, and as we were all a bit squiffy with champagne, everyone was burnt to a crisp."

Poppy gasped at the description of the fabulous night ending so tragically. Jack and Primrose looked sad and Primrose said, "My brother and our pals died that night too. We never got to see our families and tell them our marvelous news or say goodbye."

"Monty didn't mean it, darling," Jack comforted. "And now we have the opportunity to finish our dance and then get on with our eternal rest." He stared hard at Poppy. "What is your name? You do look familiar."

"I was thinking the same," laughed Poppy. "Seeing Primrose is like looking in a mirror, only she has that lovely bob haircut and mine is long. Maybe we are long lost cousins!"

Primrose hooted with giggles, "What a lark if we are connected! Please, Poppy wind the gramophone up again, we have a lot of dancing to catch up with."

Soon the little shop was ringing with the sound of jitterbug, jazz, bebop and Charleston. Jack and Primrose taught Poppy the steps and soon she was dancing as if she spent all her spare Saturday nights at the local hop. Laughter rang out; Poppy hadn't had so much fun in ages.

When they had gone through the complete repertoire of music, Jack began to look through some of the dance cards and invitations, "Primrose, look," he said, "Your mama must have packed up all last season's invitations. Wasn't that sweet? Our families were devastated, Poppy. We felt awful watching them grieve and not being able to comfort them."

Primrose suddenly shivered. "What if those ghastly people who bought the old home had burnt all our things? We would never have finished our dance and moved on."

"It's almost time to go, Poppy. Thanks so much for being such a pal, helping us finish our final dance and taking good care of our things. It has all been such fun." Primrose pealed with laughter. "Come on, Jack, the dance is over. We have just one more mystery to solve before we catch up with Monty and the others."

She paused. "I say, Poppy, invite that young man who found our trunk over for tea, see if he can dance. I think he may be able to fulfill our dream and yours. And he looks a lot like my Jack!" She blew Poppy a kiss, Jack made a half salute and the figures gradually disappeared, leaving their clothes on the floor and a faint smell of violets in the air.

Poppy felt like pinching herself. Had this evening really happened? Had she dreamed the last few hours, learning to dance as they did in the early twenties? Had she really seen ghosts or at least spirits who couldn't rest until they had completed what they'd started before their sudden tragic deaths? She was suddenly filled with unexpected delight and happiness, wondering if she had really helped these young people move on after almost ninety years. But what had Primrose meant about having another mystery to solve?

Putting dust covers carefully over all the beautiful clothes, Poppy locked up and went home to the little flat she had moved into so happily two years ago with James. James—she realized she hadn't thought of him all day. Now that was progress.

Next morning, when Poppy opened up the shop, she found a card in the door: Jason Frobisher, Builder, Renovations and Repairs. Scribbled underneath was a note. "I'd like to hear what was in the trunk. Can we meet for coffee? Call me. Jason."

Poppy heard the echo of a familiar giggle, and a smell of violets drifted round the tiny shop. "Good morning, Primrose," Poppy said. "I know you are there." She smiled in the general direction of the ceiling.

Poppy wound up the gramophone and put on the now-familiar tunes. "I wonder if Jason can dance," she mused. Picking up the phone, she dialed the number on the card. She was just about to hang up when someone answered.

"Hi, Jason, it's Poppy from the vintage shop. Is this a good time to talk?"

"No, it isn't" came a gruff reply, and the call was disconnected.

Poppy felt her heart sink. She was embarrassed, then angry at the response. He had seemed so nice and friendly. He had asked her to contact him. How could she have gotten it so wrong?

She automatically went through the process of opening the shop, feeling as if she had been doused in cold water. Since her relationship with James had finished a year or so ago, Poppy had not been out with anyone else. The emotional damage of catering to a selfish, demanding man had stopped her from being open to accepting invitations to dinner or the movies. Her friends had tried to introduce her to "suitable prospects," but she wasn't interested.

James had humiliated her. They'd spent three years together, going on holiday, finally moving in together, sharing the tiny flat she had found and made into a home for them. Then one Friday night he came home from work and told her he was moving out. They really weren't suited, she must have known that. He had found a girl he was really in love with and they were moving to London.

Poppy had been absolutely gob smacked. She had broken into sobs as the door slammed behind James and he left with his backpack, suitcases, the CDs (most of which she had bought), and the beautiful throw she had bought when they were holidaying in Spain. Maybe they had gotten into a bit of a routine, but they still had fun. What had she done wrong? It must have been her fault.

Then she remembered the long, passionate love they had made a few nights earlier. They had lingered over a beautiful dinner Poppy had prepared for their anniversary, with several bottles of his favourite wine. Afterwards they had fallen asleep in each other's arms. How could he be in love with someone else and make love to her?

It had taken ages for Poppy to begin to pick up the pieces of her life again. Her cousin Clare, who owned the vintage shop, had helped enormously. She included Poppy in outings, taking her places and out of her routine with James. Then Clare asked her to look after the shop when she went on holiday with her husband and one-year-old daughter. Poppy jumped at the chance to do something completely different. Taking unpaid leave from her administrative job at the library, she threw herself into a completely different work environment. She loved dealing with happy people who were looking for something exceptional to wear for a special party. Instead of working out statistics and updating catalogues, she enjoyed arranging racks of lovely old clothes, making sure they were clean and pressed, finding just the right outfit for the right person. Life was looking up, and she felt finally she was over James. He was just another selfish male sod.

Meeting Jason briefly, a man she'd thought was different, kind, and thoughtful, who had gone to the trouble of saving the box of beautiful clothes instead of burning them, had raised a flicker of interest. But it appeared she was wrong. Good thing she hadn't gone out with him and perhaps grown to more than like him.

Poppy filled a bucket of soapy water, pulled on rubber gloves, and began cleaning areas of the shop that hadn't been touched for a while. Like many other women, Poppy found it a good way to get rid of frustration and being made to feel inadequate—scrub everything in sight.

Several hours later, when the tiny shop was polished and cleaned to her satisfaction, she sat down with a feeling of a job well done. With a cup of coffee and a lemon poppy seed muffin to tuck into, she took a well-deserved break. Just as she had taken a most unladylike large bite, the phone rang. Emptying her mouthful into her napkin, she mumbled "Mmm! 'allo, yes?"

"Now, Poppy, that's not a very professional way to answer the phone of our select establishment." Clare's laughing voice came through the receiver.

"Oh! Clare, thank goodness it's you. I'd just taken a huge bite of a muffin and my mouth was full! And I did think it was someone else."

"Sounds interesting. This someone else wouldn't be of the male persuasion, would they? Tell me more," Clare teased.

"I'll regale you with the story when you come home. Now tell me, are you, Mike, and little Sally having fun?"

"It is so wonderful," sighed Clare, after the past few years. You are a treasure, Poppy. "Mike and I are very grateful that you stepped into the breach. This break is just what we needed; we feel renewed and reenergized. Bless you, darling. Take care and see you in a couple of weeks." The phone spluttered and Clare rang off.

Poppy felt a bit tearful when she put the phone down. She was very happy for Clare and Mike, but the conversation emphasized how alone she felt. It would be so good to have someone to talk with, who would put his arm around her and have a cuddle when life got a bit stressful. For a moment she even missed James. In the beginning he had been kind, thoughtful, and appreciative. On reflection, that hadn't lasted long. He always decided what they would do, what movies to see, and where they'd go out, and they spent time with his friends, not hers. In fact, she had been a doormat. She gave herself a little shake and reminded herself that having the wrong person in her life was not better than having no one at all.

After lunch the shop was quite busy. It was party season, and vintage clothes were all the rage. Poppy enjoyed matching the right outfit to the person who was looking for that something special.

One young woman asked, "Are you a professional stylist? My sister hired a professional who charged the earth for something gorgeous to wear to her firm's annual dinner. I think you do a much better job." She left the shop, another delighted customer.

"Yes, you are doing an amazing job," said an amused voice from behind one of the clothes racks. A tall, dark-haired man came over the counter, holding one of the outfits from Primrose and Jack's trunk. "Where did you get these clothes? These are the genuine article all right."

Poppy opened her mouth to give him an abridged version of how the clothes had come to the shop. But something stopped her. The smell of violets was in the air, and she felt protective of the young people she had danced with so energetically a few nights ago—or at least protective of their spirits.

She laughed and said, "Oh! We never reveal our sources!"

The dark eyes went cold for a moment, and then he smiled again. "Well, if you do remember or find out, I'll pay for them all. I'm a collector, and items like these are getting harder to find." He held out a simple embossed card bearing just the name Clifford Anstace and a phone number. "Anyway, I'll buy this one now. How much?" he said, reaching for his wallet.

Poppy began to tell him the price and suddenly felt a pinch. She jumped. It was the suit Jack had worn.

"I'm sorry, it isn't for sale. Someone asked me to hold it for them and I haven't got round to taking it off the rack," Poppy said firmly. Somehow she didn't want to sell Jack's suit to this man. She had taken an instant dislike to him. She wondered if it had been Primrose who pinched her.

He looked searchingly at her. Poppy knew he didn't believe her. He opened his mouth to speak but Poppy said hurriedly, "I certainly will call you if I find out from the owner where the clothes came from. Now if you don't mind, I am closing for an hour, as I have some things to sort out and I am on my own." She realized she was gabbling as she steered the man towards the door, closed it firmly, and dropped the lock.

Poppy realized she was shaking and couldn't understand why this man had disturbed her so much. She went to the rack where she had hung the clothes from the trunk, then remembered she had put them in the back room to press them. She must have forgotten Jack's suit.

Checking round the shop before closing, she wondered why the man had wanted that suit. There were at least two others of similar design, although not of the same beautiful material and style.

Suddenly she stopped what she was doing, collected all of Primrose and Jack's clothes, wrapped the gramophone up in some old clothes that wouldn't have sold, and put them in the boot of her car. Then she locked up and drove home, wondering what on earth had made her do what she did. Maybe she had inherited her Irish grandmother's intuition.

After unpacking the car and carefully storing the beautiful clothes and gramophone in her bedroom, Poppy poured a glass of Pinot Noir, popped one of the frozen dinners Clare had thoughtfully provided into the oven, and checked her answer machine. There was only one message. Nothing was said, just silence for a few moments, then the sound of a phone clicking off. Slightly unnerved, she took another sip of wine, then dismissed the message. The oven timer pinged: dinner was ready.

Next morning Poppy was singing along with the radio as she turned into the street where the vintage shop stood. She wanted to arrive early to look over some more clothes she had recently sourced. She went into shock as she saw the front door smashed and swinging open. A young constable was standing outside talking into his radio link to the station.

"What's happened?" Poppy gasped in a frightened voice. "I'm running the shop for the owners."

The young constable said, "We had a call from one of the neighbours in the new flats across the road. He noticed a car cruising up and down after you had shut the shop last evening. Early this morning he heard the sound of breaking glass, saw what was happening, and called us. He is recovering from an accident and has appointed himself 'neighbour watch.' Good job too—just as we turned into the street, we saw a car speeding off. We have a call out with the description. We haven't gone in yet as we were trying to track down the owners. Perhaps you can come in if you are up to it, and we can check if anything has been stolen." He pushed the door for Poppy and followed her into the shop.

She explained that the owners were family, and while they were away, she was looking after the business for them. She would take responsibility for enquiries as she didn't want to upset their holiday. The young constable, whose name was PC Harrison, said, "Looks like opportunists or vandals. Let us have a report if anything is missing, and I would get someone in to fix the door and lock as soon as possible." He gave her a contact number for the station, made sure Poppy felt OK to cope, and left.

Poppy sat down behind the counter, trying to think what to do next. Suddenly Jason's name popped into her head. Without thinking, she took his card from the drawer and dialed his number.

"Hello, Frobisher Renovations" came the cheery answer to the call. When he heard her voice he said, "Oh, Poppy, how good to hear from you! I thought my card had blown away when you didn't call."

"But Jason, I did call," said Poppy. "The same morning you left your card. You were quite rude and said it wasn't a good time to talk."

"It wasn't me, Poppy, honestly. I was looking forward to hearing from you. Oh, crap! Sorry for the language, but I lost or misplaced my phone for a day or two. There was some disturbance in my office and I thought it might have been stolen. Then I found it on my desk the next day, even though I was sure I had looked there. I am generally so careful with my phone—it is the link to my business." There was silence for a moment. "Maybe someone did break in and was looking for something," he said slowly.

"Jason, the shop has been broken into. The door is smashed and I am quite scared," she said, her voice trembling.

"I'll be there in ten minutes. Don't move." The phone disconnected. Ten minutes later the truck screeched to a halt outside and Jason strode in.

Poppy burst into tears and Jason put his arms around her and held her tightly. "You'll be OK. I'll fix the door, you put the kettle on. A builder can't function without his mug of tea." He grinned and gave her a quick hug. "Then we'll sit down and you can tell me all about it."

She immediately began to feel better, if a little embarrassed at having cried on his shoulder. Jason went out to fetch his tools from his truck, and she put the kettle on to make tea.

The locks replaced, mugs of tea at hand, Jason looked Poppy in the eye and said gently "Now tell me everything that's happened." Taking a sip of tea, Poppy said, "I think you are going to find it hard to believe." Taking a deep breath she told him about what had been happening since he dropped the trunk off a few days ago.

"Well I'm not sure what to think." He said slowly, "I've never encountered ghosts before on the other hand the old property I'm renovating has an interesting atmosphere. I wonder if it has something to do with the house? The suspected break in at my site office, and there have been some odd characters, nothing to do with the developer hanging round. Now the shop, and that man wanting all the clothes that came from the attic. Maybe we had better make some enquiries. I'll ask Mike if he has any idea, that's the man who bought the place from the Council when owners couldn't be found."

"I had a funny phone call or 'non' message when I got home after that man had been in the shop. I checked my answer phone at home and there was no message just a pause and the sound of the receiver being replaced. It definitely seems that something funny is going on, I am getting a bit scared." Poppy said with a shiver.

"Where do we start?" She sensed a faint smell of violets in the air and said "I think the answer might be in the trunk, I put it in the kitchen out of the way." "OK Poppy let's start I don't have to be back on site until this afternoon when I have a meeting with Mike."

Jason effortlessly picked up the trunk and put it in the middle of the shop where there was more room. Lifting the lid and admiring the beautiful condition of the trunk despite being so old, but it was empty, no secret drawers or pockets. Poppy suddenly remembered the dance cards and invitations she had found and told Jason they were in the boot of her car when she had decided to bring everything home as the visit from Mr Anstace had unsettled her. The shock of seeing the shop broken into made her forget all about them. Jason and Poppy quickly collected everything that had been in the trunk and brought them into the shop, then locked and secured the doors.

Looking through the cards and invitations Poppy came across an envelope she didn't remember seeing before. It was addressed to Poppy and Archie.

My Darling Primrose and Archie

Your father and I are devastated at your deaths and of your friends, and I don't know if we will ever recover. I know you will never read this but I feel I want to write and tell you of our plans.

We can no longer remain in the home where you grew up and we were all so happy so we are closing up the house and moving to America. Your father has a cousin who is in business in New York, and invited us to join him. We are going to try to make a life although a life without you both will be so difficult.

We have written to Mr Prichard of Prichard and Allsorp in London our Solicitors and he will keep any family papers and will know how we are getting on. With no cousins or family left in England the house will remain unsold in case we decide to return.

My darlings we hope you were happy on your last night and weren't too frightened at the end.

Your broken hearted loving Mama

Poppy brushed away a tear from her eye as she finished reading out the letter. Then she said I'm going to put a record on maybe that will help us think what to do next. Soon the sound of jazz filled the shop. A cheerful voice from behind the racks of clothes said "Good idea, darling haven't you both done well!!" The floating figures of Jack and Primrose appeared from the back of the shop. Jason grabbed Poppy and gasped, "I wasn't sure I believed in ghosts but I certainly do now!"

"The mystery is almost solved you clever things, I told you Poppy that young man of yours would help! Soon Jack and I can join our family and friends. Keep going darlings." Blowing kisses and a whiff of violets Jack and Primrose disappeared.

Jason checked the white pages on his laptop, and was astonished that there was still a company of Pritchard and Allsorp in London. He called and asked to speak with someone who dealt with old files and records. A young man called Charles Harper came on the line with a cheerful enquiry of how he could help.

After checking that the company had been in existence for over one hundred years and although there no longer had anyone with the name of Pritchard and Allsorp they retained the name as it was a symbol of confidence, success and honesty. Jason enquired if they had any files or records for a family called

Kedgley from Cheltenham who left England in the twenties after a family tragedy. After a lot of searching questions, Charles promised he would check it out and call back very soon. "I love a good *'who dun it mystery.'*" He said cheerfully.

As promised within an hour, Charles called back and sounded very excited. "I've been talking with my grandfather who was a solicitor a long time ago, he remembers the Kedgley file and his father was a friend of the family. He told me what happened and how the Kedgleys were almost destroyed by the deaths of their beloved children. I found the file and I think I should come along and discuss the contents and information about the house and a will." Poppy and Jason said they were available whenever it suited Charles and they made a time for the next day.

Jason went off for his meeting with the developer and after business had been discussed he asked Mike how he acquired the property and if there had been any problems. It turned out that the house had been abandoned for so long and despite notices in the papers no one had made a claim on the property. Land was being developed all round the house and so the Council had offered it for sale as an 'unknown and abandoned property.' He made an offer to the local authority and it was accepted. Shortly after he had a visit from a representative of a group of businessmen who wanted to bulldoze the old home and build a dozen low cost homes. He turned them down. He liked the house and thought if he renovated it had the gardens landscaped maybe a family would buy it and it would come to life again.

Problems began to plague Mike, other jobs were disrupted, staff left without notice, nothing he could report to the police but enough to cause cash flow problems. He was actually thinking of selling out as he was having increasing financial worries and the representative of the men interested in the property were becoming more aggressive.

Jason said, "Give me a couple of days Mike, I have an idea. Maybe you can give them an idea that you are seriously thinking about their offer if they would just back off for a week they'd have an answer. 'OK Jason, you have until Friday, I can't manage financially much longer if these disruptions keep occurring. I'd prefer not to sell out to these goons but I might have to."

Later the next day after Charles had left, Poppy and Jason sat speechless at what they had been told. The Kedgley family had gone to America and in partnership with his cousin, Philip Kedgley had made a fortune in the motor industry. They had another son, never returned to England although they were planning to when unexpectedly Philip had a massive heart attack at the office. Heartbroken Emily his wife died several months later.

It was only after his parents' death that Brian discovered their connection with England although he knew little. He was stunned when the solicitor advised him what he was worth. He decided to sell his share of the US family business to his cousins and travelled to England. Soon after arriving he met a beautiful girl and fell head over heels in love. They married and he settled down on the outskirts of London. He never found out about the house in Cheltenham. Brian and Rose had three children and their daughter had two daughters named Poppy and Clare.

Before he left Charles said that he was going to do some more research but it appeared that Clare and Poppy were the rightful heirs to the house. It was coming up to the statute of limitations when it would be too late to claim so he was going to hurry everything up. "My grandfather will be very pleased to hear that there is a happy ending to the sad story of his father's friends." After promising to be in touch very soon he drove away.

"What I don't understand," said Poppy, "is why that horrible man tried to buy up all the clothes and was searching for anything that might have been in the trunk?" "I think he might have had a bit of information, knew that the time to claim the house was running out and was looking for any papers or information to destroy it or pretend to be a relative and a claimant."

"Let's see if we can get Jack and Primrose back on the scene and tell them what we have found," said Poppy, putting on some jazz. The scent of violets preceded the young pair of beautiful ethereal spirits. "I knew you looked familiar Poppy, now I know why," said Primrose laughing, "to think I must be your great, great, something aunt! How marvelous – and we are both named after flowers! I knew Jason would help you solve our mystery. Thank you darlings!"

Jack said, "I feel a little sad to be leaving you both, it has been fabulous, have a happy life together I can hear some of our music being played at your wedding!" Slowly the ghosts of Primrose and Jack faded but Poppy knew they wouldn't be far away especially when they played their wonderful jazz music.

Jason put his arms around Poppy and they danced to the music which would provide wonderful memories and they began to make plans for their future.

Moonlight And Memories

"Hot," murmured Frances as her caregiver put her feet into a basin of hot water.

"Oh! Sorry, Mrs. B., I should have checked the water." Polly, a cheerful woman who came in every day to look after Frances after she had had her stroke, quickly lifted the basin away, dried her feet, then massaged soothing cream into them.

Settled again in bed and feeling warm and comfortable, Frances tried to smile at Polly but managed only a grimace. Polly understood and patted her hand. "I'll just tidy up and look in again before I leave." She picked up towels and linen to be washed, then left the room humming to herself.

Frances began to doze and suddenly a vision appeared. It was her earliest memory. There were crowds of very tall people, her mother's skirts, brass band music, cheering, and a peep of her dada smiling at her from among hundreds of other marching soldiers. She learned later that she and her mother had been waving off her dad with the Australian Imperial Army as they marched to the ships for embarkation to Gallipoli. Frances had taken off her shoes and socks and burned her feet on the sandstone pavement of Martin Place. "Hot feet," she had said as her mother pulled her through the crowds, trying to catch a glimpse of the young husband she wouldn't see again for another three years.

"OK, Mrs. B., everything is shipshape in the kitchen," Polly said. "Phyllis will be home in a few hours and I'll see you in the morning." She patted the old lady's shoulder, straightened the duvet, and left.

A familiar pain crept across Frances' chest and down her arm. She reached for her angina spray and waited for the pain to ease. She tried not to hold her breath while the discomfort subsided.

Tears of frustration for the long-gone, full, busy life she had led trickled down her face. She looked at the photographs her daughter Phyllis had placed within view: her parents, children and grandchildren, friends and family—school days, weddings, babies, graduations, all marking special events. Her eyes searched along the shelf until they stopped at a small photo of a young man seated at a piano. Lenny. He had been smiling at her as she took the photo.

The years rolled back again and the music of Benny Goodman and Louis Armstrong echoed in her memory. She was seventeen and at the local dance hall with her girlfriends. For some reason she had been full of excitement that day, with the feeling that something wonderful was about to happen. She felt the world was at her feet and she could do and be anything she wanted. Laughing and jitterbugging with the girls and some of the young men she knew from the neighbourhood, Frances became aware of someone watching her—the piano player. He smiled, lifted his hand from the keyboard, and gave her a little wave.

Soon after, she felt a hand on her arm and a voice said, "Can I have this dance? I'm on a break." She felt the excitement of the unknown run through her veins as she nodded her acceptance. "I'm Lenny. I've seen you here before and wanted to meet you. I hoped you would spare me a dance." He smiled a heartbreaking smile and they danced together as if they already knew each other's steps. Too soon he had to go back on stage again.

"Wait for me when the evening finishes. I have to talk with you. Please?"

He gazed into her eyes and she answered, "Yes."

Frances told her friends not to wait for her, as she would catch the last bus home. They weren't keen on leaving her, but she was determined. "I'll be OK. See you at church tomorrow morning."

She sat at a table near the stage, and as it got later and the band still played, she got a little nervous, wondering if she would miss her bus. When it was nearly midnight, Frances decided she had better run for the bus. She couldn't wait for Lenny anymore. She gathered up her coat and bag, but turning to go, she felt a hand on her arm and a voice in her ear. "Not leaving, Frankie, are you?" said Lenny.

"I have to. If I miss the last bus I'll get in trouble," stammered Frances.

"I'll walk you home. I want to see you again and get to know you." He picked up her coat, put it around her shoulders, took her hand, and guided her out through the last of the dancing crowd.

It was a beautiful Sydney evening. A full moon hung low in the sky, a light breeze blew in from the harbour and the young couple gazed at each other, knowing they were beginning something extraordinary. Lenny took her hand, tucked it into his elbow, gazed into her eyes, and said, "Which way is home, Frankie?"

As they strolled along the waterfront, they gazed in amazement at the rising Sydney Harbour Bridge and the two spans which had been joined that month. All too soon they reached Paddington, where Frances lived. She looked anxiously towards the house. "I have to go. I've never been out this late before. My mum and dad will be very angry if they are awake."

"I'll watch to see you are safely inside. Wave to me from your window and then I'll go. When can we meet again? We are playing again next Saturday at the dance hall. You will be there, won't you?" Lenny asked, holding her hand tightly.

"Yes, if I can," she said. He kissed her cheek and she ran quietly towards the back door, which was generally left unlocked. Soon after, she leaned out of her bedroom window and blew Lenny a kiss.

Her sister, Maggie, stirred as Frances pulled the blanket back. "Sshh! Go to sleep," Frances whispered as she climbed into bed.

The week crawled by. Frances went to work and fielded questions from her friends about the piano player. One evening when she arrived home from work, her dad was sitting on the veranda. He called, "Hey, Frances, come and talk with your old dad for a while."

"I'll just say hello to Mum. Shall I bring you a beer, Dad?"

"Thanks, Frances, you're a good girl." Dad lit up another cigarette.

When Frances had come outside and poured her dad's beer, they sat for a while looking out over the garden.

"Well, Frances, when are you going to tell me about your young man?" asked her dad, smiling while at the same time trying to look severe.

"What young man?" Frances stalled.

"The young man who kept you out late last Saturday night. The one who watched while you got inside safely." He smiled. "I figured if he was that thoughtful, he might just be a considerate young man."

"You never said anything. I—I thought you were asleep," stuttered Frances.

"When my daughter is home safely, then I go to sleep. I trust you, but you can't always trust the young men around today."

Frances and her dad talked until Mum called them for dinner. "Before we go in, Frances, I have something for you," Dad said. He handed her a camera. "It's called a Beaux Box Brownie, the latest thing. I did some work for a photographer today and he didn't have the cash to pay me, so he offered me this. He said it was brand new and took fantastic pictures. I thought you might like to have it. Take pictures of the family and maybe your young man too."

Frances threw her arms around his neck. "Thanks, Dad, I'll take some great photos! And the first will be of you. Smile!" She pointed the little box and pressed the button.

The following Saturday, she took a photo of Lenny sitting at the piano at the dance. But three months later, Lenny was dead. Coming home late from a wedding the band had played at, Joe, the drummer, had fallen asleep at the wheel. The van crashed, killing both Joe and Lenny. Francis was heartbroken.

Seventy years later, Frances lay in bed dozing, pictures and memories running through her head. Working and laughing with her husband, Pete, and their three children. Her parents, brothers and sister, cousins and friends. Half-forgotten memories jumped like a film reel that had jammed.

Then it all slowed down. Music drifted into the room and she saw herself at seventeen in her favourite yellow dress, dancing with Lenny, her arms round his neck. She heard his voice reassuring her, "It's all going to be OK, Frankie." In the background she could see her mum and dad. There was a smell of frangipani just like the tree in their garden of the old house in Paddington. Pete and his family were there, and her brothers and sister, who had died years ago. They were all smiling and young again.

Frances relaxed and let the warm feeling of being loved wash over her. She closed her eyes and slipped into a deep sleep.

Phyllis arrived home an hour or so after her mother's heart had stopped. When she got over the shock, she realized that her mum was smiling, her face smooth and anxiety-free. She couldn't understand why there was a smell of frangipani in the room.

Weekend In Russell

"I don't know how to thank you, Maggie, you really are a dear, good friend," said Rosalie as she got up to leave.

"Nonsense, Rosalie! You are always there for me and everyone else. You've saved my sanity with tea and by seeing the funny side of any problem over the years; now it is your turn. Off you go, and enjoy that restful weekend before you get caught up in rush-hour traffic!"

Rosalie gazed at the dark little head of her son, Tim, and the bright red hair of his friend, Michael. The two were completely engrossed in a complicated game which only four-year-old best friends could understand. She knew he would be happy and secure with Maggie, Maggie's husband, Joe, and their three children.

A quick hug all round and off she went, a few tears moistening her eyes. It was the first time she had left Tim for more than one night.

A weekend in Russell! Alone! Rosalie couldn't quite believe it. She loved Tim dearly, but to have a few days without the constant demands on her attention, to relax and walk by herself, would be wonderful. She had been so tired lately and had been getting tense and irritated with everyone at work and even her darling son. Maggie had planted the idea of a few days away and then dismissed all her objections until Rosalie finally agreed. Now here she was, driving over the Auckland Harbour Bridge on her way north at last.

As she drove, the memory of her last impromptu weekend away made her smile. Her husband, Richard, had arrived home early one Friday and said in that irrepressible way of his, "We're off on a magical mystery tour. Pack the bags, Tim's nappies, and let's go!"

An hour later, with Tosca the dog and Charlie the cat farmed out to Maggie and Joe, the house was locked up and she was ushered laughing to the car, where eighteen-month-old Tim was already strapped into his safety seat. They drove down to the beautiful Coromandel Peninsula in the Bay of Plenty.

It had been a magical three days. They had made love under the stars, talked and laughed as they had before the arrival of Tim and a mortgage. At the little holiday home where they stayed in Cook's Beach, the owner's daughter had taken a shine to Tim. She played and looked after him all weekend. Richard and Rosalie returned to Auckland on Sunday refreshed and rejuvenated, promising each other they wouldn't let the pressure of everyday living stop them from putting aside some time each week to talk and catch up with each other on what they were thinking and feeling. To solve any worries before they became problems.

The memory of that weekend comforted Rosalie during the dark time after Richard's death. He'd been coming home from working late at the computer centre when a drunk driver lost control of his vehicle, veered across the motorway, and smashed into Richard's car. Richard was killed instantly. Another statistic, another victim of the culture of drinking and driving. Two years later Rosalie still shivered when she thought of those awful months of coping and coming to terms that her best friend, her lover, husband, and Tim's daddy, wouldn't be coming home.

The road north was fairly clear and she made good time, stopping for a rest and coffee in Whangarei before pressing on to Russell.

"Hello, men," said Joe to Michael and Tim as he arrived home from work. After distributing hugs, swings, and pats to children and dogs respectively, he planted a kiss on his wife's head and sat down at the kitchen bench to exchange news of the day.

"Rosie get away OK?" he asked Maggie.

Maggie smiled at her tall, skinny, red-haired husband, whom she loved dearly but who at times could drive her to distraction when he forgot time and got involved with one of his "projects" in the garage, disappearing for hours at a time.

"Oh, yes. After checking six times that Tim had everything he possibly might need for the weekend, plus a surprise for the boys if they get fretful, and a bottle of wine for us in case we got fretful! She is a dear." Maggie smiled and finished preparing dinner while Joe set the table.

"Did you tell her Philip would be there?" asked Joe.

"Mmm...well, no, not exactly."

"That means no. Well, I hope they get on better this time if they do meet. I won't forget that dinner party in a hurry. I don't know which one of them was in a worse temper. If one of them had said something was black, the other would have sworn it was white."

"Well," said Maggie with spirit, "I think if they got to know each other, they really would enjoy each other's company. It shouldn't be allowed—two good-looking, intelligent, kind people who have both lost someone they loved dearly, being alone. I know they would be good for each other. Anyway, Philip is far too attractive—at least he is when he smiles—to be let loose on those calculating females in his office. Rosalie is just right for him, you'll see." All the same, Maggie was slightly apprehensive about the reaction if the "accidental" meeting didn't work out.

"Philip is certainly taking a long time to get over Claire's dumping him for Karl. Just because the Swiss gnome had bank accounts in five different countries, three houses, and a yacht. I think Philip was obsessed with Claire. Those types of females are too hot to handle." Joe gave his wife a cuddle. "I am so glad I have a wife who completely understands me." They were giggling when Josie, their oldest child, bounded in and demanded dinner as she was "starving."

About an hour later, Rosalie telephoned to say she had arrived safely and was settled into the Duke of Marlborough Hotel; she wasn't too tired and was just going to get something to eat. Maggie reassured her Tim was very happy and said Joe was reading the children a bedtime story.

Next morning, after a deep, dreamless night's sleep, Rosalie woke without that awful tired feeling she had been experiencing these past few months. Going to the window, she pulled the curtains to let in a beautiful, sunshine-filled morning. The bay sparkled, yachts bobbed on the water, and people strolled in shorts and tee shirts; it must be warm. Quickly she stepped into the shower, got dressed, and hurried down for breakfast, eager to be on her way to explore the old township.

The dining room was about half full, and from the accents she could pick out, there were Americans, Japanese, and Europeans, all laughing and talking. She sat down and smiled at the person at the next table, a young man with fair, sun-bleached hair and skin brown as a suntan lotion advertisement.

"Good morning, wonderful day," he said in a gentle Southern American accent.

Rosalie ordered her breakfast, was soon finished, and went on her way. As she passed her American neighbour's table, he said, "Have a nice day," and for once she was not irritated by the remark. It sounded as if he genuinely meant it, and it was as if she had never heard the glib comment before.

Collecting the bag containing her sunglasses, jacket, and book, off she went, feeling really good, relaxed, and slightly guilty, as if she was playing truant from life. She strolled down to the wharf where boats, yachts, and the ferry from Paihia across the bay were tied up. Looking into the sparkling clear water, she was amazed to see hundreds of tiny and not-so-tiny fish darting around. Half a dozen small boys and girls sat with fishing lines dangling over the side of the wharf and the squeals of delight from the young fishermen as they caught another fish brought a smile to her face.

"They are having as much fun catching their fish as the man who caught that 110-kilo swordfish on the weighting block," said a deep voice a few yards away.

Rosalie looked up with astonishment at the tall figure leaning on the wharf railing. The voice seemed vaguely familiar.

"Philip Ashton. We met about two months ago at Maggie and Joe's," said the tall, dark-haired man. His eyes were hidden behind sunglasses. He smiled and his face took on a completely different appearance. The closed-in, defensive look disappeared.

Hmm! He is quite good-looking after all. Maggie was right, said Rosalie to herself. Out loud she replied, "Oh! Yes, Philip, I remember. I am afraid I wasn't very good company that evening. Life had been rather stressful and Maggie thought I needed cheering up. I didn't contribute much sparkling conversation that evening." She smiled and held out her hand. She was unprepared for the tingling shock as a warm, firm hand grasped hers. Putting on her sunglasses to hide her confusion, she asked, "And what are you doing here?"

"Well, I have been rather tense lately—barking at my poor secretary, working long hours—and then I fell victim to one of the virus floating around and couldn't seem to shake it off. Joe recommended I come up here for some rest and recuperation. How about you?"

"Mmm, something along the same lines as you, only it was Maggie who made the recommendation."

Both were silent for a moment, and then burst out laughing. "Maggie's matchmaking," they said together, smiling at each other.

"Do you mind?" he asked. "We could have some fun exploring together and I would enjoy your company, now that both of us have improved our tempers!"

"Not at all," said Rosalie. "I'm glad to have someone to talk to, as long as it isn't about the cost of living or how soon the statistics report will be completed! Russell certainly is a welcome change from Auckland."

They strolled off towards Pompalier House, built in 1841. They spoke tentatively at first, then gradually relaxed. The house's beautiful old-fashioned garden, the bees buzzing around the blossoms, the heady perfume of the flowers, and a gentle breeze through the trees created a magical atmosphere where they strolled, sometimes talking, sometimes not.

In a hidden corner of the garden, they both bent to smell a rose and gently bumped heads. Rosalie felt her cheeks blush as their eyes met. She felt a long-forgotten churning in the pit of her stomach and had difficulty steadying her pounding heart. Surely he must notice. To hide her confusion, she turned away and pretended to look at the herb garden. It was so long since Richard had held her and loved her. She missed his closeness and warmth. She took some deep breaths and, composed again, turned and smiled at Philip, who was following her down the path.

They had a wonderful day exploring the township. They visited the oldest surviving church in New Zealand, built in 1836, complete with walls scarred from musket balls from one of the many skirmishes the early pioneers had contended with. Arts and crafts shops had sprung up in recent years, run by people from many countries, who considered the rest of the world well lost for life in beautiful Russell in New Zealand's Bay of Islands.

After lunching on grilled fresh fish pulled from the water a few hours earlier, accompanied by a wonderfully light local Pinot Gris, they found a quiet spot on the beach under a pohutukawa tree and talked and talked. For the first time, Philip talked in depth of how Claire had hurt him. He described how much he had loved her and how devastated he had been when he discovered she was cheating on him with a Swiss financier she had met while on a fashion shoot in Milan. Arriving home from a business trip to Sydney two years ago, he'd found a letter propped up on the drinks trolley: "*It has been wonderful, darling, but time to move on. Karl can offer so much more in Europe for my career. No hard feelings. Ciao, Claire.*"

"I was shattered," said Philip. "I hadn't realized how vulnerable I was and I vowed it would never happen again. I buried myself in my work." He looked closely at the slim, pretty woman who sat listening sympathetically. She didn't offer platitudes, just squeezed his hand, and he felt that she understood how lost he had felt.

"Do you know," he said in amazement, "that is the first time in two years I have talked about Claire without a knife twisting in my gut? I think I am cured!" leaned over and brushed his lips lightly over Rosalie's cheek. She jumped as if burnt. Philip put his arm round her and said, "Don't worry, we'll take it slowly. Now tell me all about you. You have been listening to me for the last hour or so—it's your turn now."

Hesitantly, Rosalie began to talk of how she and Richard had met in Australia seven years ago when they were both on holiday. They had travelled around Australia and returned to New Zealand to marry. Tim was born exactly nine months later and they were so happy, working hard on the tiny house they had bought, planning their lives, until that fateful night when a drunk driver had wiped out all their plans and Richard's life.

She tried to explain her feelings of anger at the unfairness of it all. The drunk driver had escaped with a broken wrist and a fine. Richard had been going to see an insurance broker to arrange life insurance; the appointment was for the week following his death. It had broken her heart to have to go back to work and leave Tim in a daycare centre. Maggie cared for him two days a week, but Rosalie couldn't expect her friend to have him all the time. Maggie had enough to do with Josie at school, Michael the same age as Tim, and baby Megan, now nine months old. As she talked, tears began to flow. Philip was upset that she was so distressed.

"Don't worry," she sniffed. "I'm fine, really. I feel as if a plug has been pulled on all the emotions I've bottled up over the last two years. It's as if a stone has been lifted from my heart and all the sadness is drifting away. Thanks,

Philip, for listening. I haven't been able to talk to anyone else like this, not even Maggie."

He leaned over and kissed her again, this time gently on the lips. They tasted salty from her tears. Holding each other tightly for a few minutes while catching their breath, each felt the other's heart beating wildly.

"Come on," he said huskily. "I think it is time we got moving. The sun is going down. There is a great little restaurant on the waterfront. I'll try and get a table while you get changed."

They walked back to the hotel. Philip kissed her forehead and held her tightly. "To think I nearly didn't come on this weekend break. What would I have done if our paths hadn't crossed again?" He gently pushed her towards the stairs.

Rosalie's heart sang as she ran upstairs. She stopped and looked back. Philip had just turned away, and she stood and admired his body in his well-fitting jeans and beautifully tailored casual shirt. He turned and caught her watching him and they grinned at each other. She blew a kiss and went to her room.

She turned on the taps of the deep old-fashioned tub and poured in two sachets of bubble bath. There was an hour and half to get ready. Lovely—time to relax and think. As the fragrant water soothed her body, Rosalie thought of the day. How different from the dinner party at Joe and Maggie's, when they had been two stressed-out individuals who couldn't stand the sight of each other. She laughed and raised the glass of wine she had treated herself to from the mini bar. "Thanks, Maggie!"

Just after seven p.m., she was dressed and walked down the stairs to the hotel lobby. Thank heavens she had brought her one good dress, a floaty rainbow of colours with a matching scarf. Rosalie felt wonderful in it, and she blessed the day she had bought it in a sale and put off paying the telephone bill for another week. Philip walked in, looking elegant and handsome in beautifully tailored trousers and jacket. When he saw Rosalie walking down the stairs, his smile broke out, transforming his remote features. He walked over, took her hand, and kissed her on the cheek.

"You are so beautiful!" He smiled. "I am the happiest man in Russell to be escorting you and have your company." They strolled out into the balmy evening, and admiring glances followed the attractive couple.

Philip said, "The restaurant is an old converted colonial cottage, and the food the best this side of Ponsonby, I've been told. Our table won't be ready until eight. Are you warm enough for a stroll along the wharf?"

"Yes, thank you, I feel wonderful. The weather is amazing, arranged especially for us." Rosalie smiled.

Philip suddenly laughed and said, "Do you think Maggie arranged the weather too?" He pointed out over the bay at the most glorious red-gold full moon rising above the horizon. Neither had seen one like it before. It seemed close enough to touch, and the moonlight reflected on the water made a path across the gently lapping waves straight to where they stood at the end of the wharf. They stood wrapped in the magic of the evening, while music from the hotel, cafes, and nearby moored yachts drifted along the beach.

Turning towards each other, they both knew this was a moment in their lives they would never forget. Their kisses were no longer tentative and gentle, but passionate, full of longing, exploring. They leaned for support or the wharf rail. He kissed the pulse in her throat and she twisted her fingers through his hair.

And so began the most romantic evening of Rosalie's life. She felt cherished and cared for; they laughed and talked easily as if they had known each other for ever. The waitress gave them special attention, and the other diners looked with interest at the couple who were oblivious to anyone else, and smiled at the atmosphere that enveloped the lovers. At midnight they were the last people in the little restaurant. Philip had been right—the food was delicious and accompanied by the perfect wine. Before they asked for the bill, the owner and his one waitress joined them with a special bottle of port that Harry kept for customers he felt deserved the best.

"You two have spread a little magic here tonight. You've earned a glass of this very good port. Tell me what you think—or do you prefer a brandy?"

The port was superb and finished off a perfect evening. Harry told them stories of customers from all over the world who took some time out of life to recharge their batteries in Russell. The men who owned land in the Bay of Islands, European and American multimillionaires, said they felt they owned a little piece of paradise. From time to time they appeared for a few weeks to recover from the stresses of high-pressure business, to relax, do a little fishing, and escape from deadlines and demands.

Rosalie and Philip finally said good night to their host, promising to return. They walked slowly back to the hotel, a little heady with the wine, the atmosphere, and the evening. On one side of the path were little cottages, a museum, and native trees and flowers, and on the other the dark blue water edged with lacy white foam splashed gently on the sand.

At the door of the Duke of Marlborough, Philip kissed her gently on her nose. "Off to bed. We've had an incredible day; get some sleep and I will pick you up after breakfast." He hugged her briefly. "If I stay here, I'll ravish you on the steps of this staid and correct hotel." He patted her bottom and said, "Sleep well my darling. See you tomorrow after breakfast."

Rosalie ran upstairs, fumbled with her key in the lock, and hurried to the window to see him disappear in the direction of his motel. As she prepared for bed, she guiltily realized she had hardly thought of Tim all day, except when she was telling Philip about him. Still, Maggie would have phoned if anything was wrong.

Contrary to what she expected, Rosalie was soon asleep. Just before she woke at dawn, she dreamed of Richard. He was standing under a tree with sunlight behind him, smiling that crooked smile she loved. "Goodbye, Rosie my love," he said. "You are going to be fine now."

The image faded until he disappeared. Rosalie woke with a start, and with amazing clarity she felt a chapter in her life was finished, and a new one beginning.

From the window she saw that the weather had deteriorated a little from yesterday, but it still was a wonderful day. Soon she would see Philip. At eight o'clock she was eating breakfast when her tanned American neighbour from yesterday appeared and asked if he could join her. Rosalie felt so happy she said, "Certainly, please do." He told her his name was Dave, and he soon had her laughing at his grossly exaggerated stories of life crewing on a yacht which so far had been sailing round the world for two years. He was staying at the Duke of Marlborough Hotel while waiting for his next crewing job. Dave had dropped out of his father's business in Dallas, Texas, and didn't miss the high-pressure business life at all.

"Only thing missing is a lovely lady like you to share my hammock," he teased, lifting her hand to his lips to plant a lingering kiss.

Just then Rosalie noticed Philip standing white-faced in the doorway of the dining room. Her head had been thrown back as she laughed at Dave's outrageous flirting.

Philip turned on his heel and stormed out. Rosalie ran after him and caught up with him on the path leading away from the hotel.

"Philip, what's wrong?" she asked.

"I might have known. You can't trust any woman. Did you sleep with him last night after you left me?" he snarled with a face like thunder.

"How dare you!" she raged, almost in tears. "He is just a funny young man whose second nature is to flirt, and if you are so untrusting, I never want to see you again!" Rosalie rushed off in the direction of the hotel and dashed up the stairs, ignoring Dave, who called after her.

She couldn't believe what had happened. Distraught, she threw a few things in a bag. Hearing footsteps on the stairs, she rushed to her window, threw it open, and stepped out onto the fire escape, then climbed down to the ground. She ran down the beach in the opposite direction of where she and Philip had strolled so happily yesterday.

Sobbing, she climbed over the rocks around the bays, not knowing where she was going. She just wanted to find somewhere to be alone so she could try and make sense of Philip's dreadful reaction to her talking to another man.

Walking and climbing over the rocks, her mind and emotions churning, Rosalie didn't notice the sky darken. A storm was brewing and the tide was coming in. As the first heavy drops of rain started falling, she looked up at the sky, missed her footing, and slipped. Her right foot caught firmly between two sharp rocks. The rain poured down and the sea, so beautiful and calm yesterday, looked grey and menacing. As she desperately tried to free her foot, Rosalie felt the first splash of the sea as the tide crept nearer.

"Help, help! Oh please, someone help me!" she cried. But there was no one to hear except the sea gulls crying above her. Strangely, she remembered her Irish great aunt telling her sea gulls were the spirits of sailors who had drowned. Before she drifted into unconsciousness from fear and the pain in her foot, she wondered if her spirit would become a sea gull.

"Rosie, Rosie!" She heard her name in the distance and then strong arms supporting her. She opened her eyes to find Philip holding her tightly, grim faced, while Dave chipped frantically at the rocks trapping her foot, trying to see under the water where she was trapped.

"Philip—" she began.

"Don't talk," he ordered. "Just concentrate on helping us get you out of here."

Dave wrenched her foot from the loosened rocks before the next wave crashed over them. "The ankle bone looks broken, Phil," he said. "We'll have to carry her."

Heavens, thought Rosalie, *Philip looks so angry. I expect he doesn't want to have anything to do with me anymore.* Emotional and in pain, she felt tears slip down her face. Philip paused briefly in helping Dave move the rocks so they could get out of danger, kissed her fiercely, and said, "Don't be frightened, we'll get you out."

In spite of her fear, the pain in her foot, and the fact that she was up to her waist in water, her heart began to lighten. "I expect this will make a great story to entertain your girls in different ports—rescuing a silly damsel in distress!" Rosalie said to Dave with a little smile, trying to lighten the drama.

"Certainly will, princess," said the chirpy American. "OK, Phil, we'd better try and get on our way. That foot looks pretty bad."

Philip caught her up and for a moment held her tightly in his strong arms, too emotional to move. "I was so afraid we wouldn't be able to get you free," he muttered against her hair.

"Come on, you love birds, let's get going before we are all drowned!" Dave hurried them along, timing each rock climb to when the waves receded. Somehow, between them and with Rosalie helping as much as she could, they clambered over the rocks towards Russell and safety.

Later that afternoon, Rosalie was tucked up in bed. The doctor had just left after strapping her ankle, ordering rest and no rock-climbing in the near future! Philip put his head round the door. "Can I come in?" he asked.

Rosalie blushed, remembering him carrying her up the stairs, taking her wet clothes off, and putting her in a hot bath, tenderly washing and drying her, trying not to bump the injured ankle. He'd tucked her up warmly in bed just as the local doctor arrived.

"Philip, please come in and tell me how you found me. And why was Dave with you?"

Philip looked uncomfortable. "I'll never forgive myself for such a stupid reaction when I saw you and Dave together. When I saw him kissing your hand, I immediately saw Karl kissing Claire's hand the first time I caught them together, and my mind just boiled over in a black rage. Will you ever forgive me?"

Rosalie held out her arms, and twenty minutes later, when they had kissed thoroughly, he gathered he was forgiven.

A gentle knocking on the door brought them down to earth. Philip opened the door and Dave popped his head around. "Just had to see what the doc said and if you are going to be OK, princess," he said.

Rosalie assured him she was much better. "I can see that," he said, grinning slyly at Philip and causing her to blush again. "I shan't interrupt; you two obviously have lots to talk about. I've asked the desk to send up some hot soup, toast, and a bottle of brandy."

"Thank you, Dave, you have been wonderful. Thank you so much," said Rosalie sleepily. She felt the warmth of the blankets, heard the howling gale outside, and tried not to think what would have happened if the two men hadn't found her.

"Thanks, Dave," Philip said. "I'll buy you a drink later when Rosalie has gone to sleep. You saved not only her life but mine as well."

Dave blew a kiss to Rosalie, grinned at Philip, and went downstairs. The soup, toast, and brandy arrived. The waitress set the table close to the bed, and after making sure they had everything they needed, she closed the door gently behind her.

With a bowl of delicious chicken soup inside them and a tot of brandy at hand, Philip began to tell Rosalie how they had found her. "Dave found me prowling around outside. After he had given me his version of your breakfast together and told me not to be such a damn fool, we discovered that you had disappeared. The porter told me he saw you climbing down the fire escape and going off in the direction of the rocks. When the weather started changing, Dave said he would come with me to look for you. Thank God he did."

He paused to kiss her again and then continued the story. "We set off round the rocks. With the changing weather and the tide coming in, we were really worried. I was getting desperate when we couldn't find you, and then we heard a faint cry. I wasn't sure if it was you or the sea gulls. Someone must have been guiding us, because another twenty minutes and it might have been too late."

Rosalie had a sudden mental picture of her dream of Richard. *Goodbye*, he'd said. *You're going to be fine now.*

"Precious girl," Philip said, "I know we haven't known each other very long if you count the days, but I feel we have known each other forever. Can you imagine spending your life with a sometimes hot-tempered idiot?" He looked fierce and tense again.

"Oh, Philip darling…what about Tim? Are you really sure? I get quite stroppy myself from time to time. Could you put up with me?" She gazed up at him from her pillows.

"I can't stand it anymore," growled Philip. "I'm coming in beside you." He locked the door, pulled the heavy drapes, turned down all the lights but a gentle lamp beside the bed, stripped off his clothes, and slipped in beside her. He put his arms around her and she lost her breath as she felt his hard body against hers. "Now, my girl, if it wasn't for your ankle, we'd be making mad passionate love. As it is, we'll have to make the best of it." He kissed her hard again. "I'm waiting for an answer. Can you imagine spending the rest of your life with me, Tim, and all the other children we are going to have?"

"I think I'd better say yes—although we might have to have a discussion about how many other children. But I can't remember the last time when something felt so right. I feel as if I have come home."

Their lips met tenderly. Sweetly they nuzzled each other's faces and necks, inhaling the scent of their skin. Philip caressed her body and she felt it come alive. "Lie still," he commanded softly. "I want to know you and for you to feel everything. Don't move, don't think, just feel."

Beginning with her eyelids, he gently kissed and nibbled her body, slowly exploring, discovering her warmth and pushing away her arms that reached hungrily for him. "I told you to just feel. I love you so much, my darling; I want to show you how much."

Rosalie surrendered to the overwhelming rush of pounding blood, the incredible sureness of his hands on her body. His lips on her breast brought her to where she felt she was floating outside herself. "Please, Philip, now," she begged. Her arms grasped his body closer and they were locked together, at last fulfilling the hunger and desire that had been building between them over the past few days. The storm raged outside, an accompaniment to the passion overwhelming the lovers within.

Next morning, drowsy with the drama of the day before and the wonderful release of pent-up emotion for them both, Rosalie lay with her head on Philip's shoulder while they made plans for travelling back to Auckland, having her car collected; and their future together.

"Shall we play Maggie and Joe at their own game?" said Philip with a grin. "I'll phone and pretend their plan was a disaster."

Back in Auckland, Maggie and Joe were laughing at Michael and Tim, who were playing zoo keepers and feeding building blocks to Megan through the bars of her playpen. "Well," said Maggie, "I suppose she does look like a tiger in her orange-striped baby suit. Joe, there's the phone. Answer it, will you, honey?"

"Hello, Auckland Zoo," said Joe cheerfully.

A sharp voice came over the line. "Joe, it's Philip."

Joe put his hand over the mouthpiece and hissed to Maggie, "It's Philip." Maggie quickly put her ear to the other side of the phone.

"Yes, Philip, how has your weekend been?" Joe began.

Philip interrupted in a bad-tempered tone, "What do you mean by not telling me your irritable neighbour was going to be up here? She has completely disrupted my restful weekend! I have a bone to pick with you and Maggie. I'll call in on the way home this evening."

"Oh! Right-o, Phil, see you later, then." Joe hung up with a groan. "He will be unbearable next week. That's torn it."

"Hmm. I don't know so much," said Maggie thoughtfully "I'm sure I heard someone giggling in the background, and I am certain I heard kissing noises! I wonder…?"

Originally from the Glens of Antrim, Northern Ireland, Robyn P. Murray attributes growing up in this mythical land to her love of reading and writing stories. Robyn began her world travels at eighteen, visiting New Zealand and then moving to Germany, where she worked for Reuters and Time Life during the exciting Cold War era.

Her travels have also taken her to Europe and North Africa, but for the past forty years, she has lived in New Zealand. She has a son and two grandsons and recently published two children's books—one of which was translated into braille for children with visual impairments.

Over the years, she has intermittently written fiction and nonfiction and been published in magazines. She has read her work and the work of other writers on radio and regularly reads to children at early childhood centers and primary schools.

ACKNOWLEDGEMENT

Thank you to my family the past generations and
special thanks to my sisters Ann and Pauline.

Printed in Great Britain
by Amazon.co.uk, Ltd.,
Marston Gate.